A
DANGEROUS
OBSERVER

A DANGEROUS OBSERVER

AMANDA DEWEES

Acknowledgments

A Dangerous Observer is one of the most ambitious books I've ever tackled, and there were times when I feared it would never get written at all. I want to thank the friends who helped me through the long process of planning and writing it, especially Lisa Blackwell, Krista Chafin-Raney, Maurice Cobbs, Caitlyn Trautwein, and Charles R. Rutledge. Copious thanks go to my marvelous beta readers, Darrell Z. Grizzle and Peyton Smith-Hopman, and to Heather Johnson, whose clever suggestion about character inspiration helped me rediscover my excitement for the project at a time when it was flagging.

During my research I consulted Bella Bathurst's terrific book *The Wreckers*, which I highly recommend to anyone interested in this fascinating subject.

Books by Amanda DeWees

Cursed Once More: The Sequel to With This Curse
A Dangerous Observer
The Heir of Hawksclaw (novella)
Sea of Secrets
With This Curse

Sybil Ingram Victorian mysteries:
Nocturne for a Widow
The Last Serenade
A Haunting Reprise
"Christmas at Gravesend" (short story)
"Spectral Strains" (short story)

Victorian Vampires novellas:
As Vital as Blood
As Strong as Earth

The Ash Grove Chronicles
(young adult paranormal romance):
"On Shadowed Wings" (short story)
The Shadow and the Rose
Casting Shadows
Among the Shadows

A husband without faults is a dangerous observer.

—George Saville, 1688

CHAPTER ONE
Cecily (1860)

Connor Blake had saved her life, plain and simple. Without him—well, she would have been ruined, utterly ruined.

But that night at the ball when she had stood staring at Freddie Hightower, numb with shock as the horrible words rang in her ears, she had not at first known that rescue was at hand.

"We cannot marry?" she repeated.

Freddie still held her hand, and now he squeezed it as if to reassure her. His earnest blue eyes gazed into hers in what looked like an anxious appeal that she would understand...and not make a scene. In this alcove they were mere steps away from the rest of the company. With part of her mind she resented him for giving her the news in a public setting. It forced her to be discreet in her response and do nothing that would draw attention—such as, for example, kicking him in the shins.

"Father says it is impossible until I turn twenty-one. But that is only two years—"

"Two *years!*" How could she and Cousin Margaret survive that long? They had spent what little money they had on Cecily's clothes for this Season. Some days they had nothing to eat except the collation at the night's ball. Cecily was all too aware that she had gained a reputation as a flibbertigibbet because she sometimes broke into a peal of laughter seemingly for no reason when she needed to cover the rumbling in her belly.

"Why didn't they tell you this before now?" she demanded. "Why would they wait all Season?"

"I thought they had no objection. I was mistaken." Now his eyes wavered and dropped. He was not being truthful with her. Perhaps he had not told his parents how serious his regard for her was.

And meanwhile, all Season, everyone had taken their engagement as fact. Including Cecily herself, for Freddie had from the very beginning pursued her with a single-minded devotion that made other suitors drop away, certain they stood no chance.

Not, she forced herself to admit, that there had been many other suitors once her poverty came to light. Sooner or later everyone realized that the fair-haired eighteen-year-old had nothing more to her name than a pretty face, a cheerful disposition, and a gift for charades. Freddie Hightower alone had not been discouraged. He seemed truly to love her, and that selfless devotion won her heart. How could she fail to respond to a man so noble, so pure of heart?

Yet it was this man who was failing her now. "What would happen if we married without your parents' permission?" she ventured. "They would come around, wouldn't they, given time?"

His expression of horror would have been answer enough, but he stammered, "I'd have nothing—we'd have nothing, you understand. They would strip me of my income. We would be as poor as church mice."

She knew all too well what it was like to have nothing, to swallow her pride and live off of the charity of others, and was reluctant to continue thus even with masculine protection. But there was one glimmer of a possibility raised by his words. "You told me there was a time when you thought of going into the church," she began.

He actually drew away from her as if the words were contagion. "I could never make do on so pitiful an income," he said. "I certainly could not afford to keep a wife. Dearest, there is nothing for it but to wait. In two years' time—"

In two years' time she would have fallen into complete obscurity as a governess, if anyone would have so ignorant a girl to teach their children...and if any matron would hire someone pretty enough to draw her husband's eye. She would be out on the street. Factory work? She felt she would die if she had to live in squalid poverty, sharing a privy with a dozen families, working fifteen hours a day over machinery that might maim her if she wasn't careful.

The alternative, she knew, was to be kept by some wealthy man. But she shrank from the degradation of letting her body be handled by the kind of men who would set her up in such an arrangement. She thought of the men whose eyes lingered on her, who tried to make her blush with remarks she understood only as far as she recognized their insinuating tone, and pushed back nausea. Even if she happened to catch the eye of someone not entirely repellent, she would be cut off from the world as her social circle drew in to contain only other mistresses. And she might be cast off at any moment; there was no certainty of the future.

She had only one other card to play, though she knew it would shock him. "Could we not tell them we *must* marry?" she asked. "If they thought a grandchild was on the way—"

He dropped her hand as if it were a scorpion. "Cecily! How the blazes can you suggest such a thing?"

Now on top of everything else she had lost his respect. "I am sorry," she said miserably, "but you don't understand how difficult—how really difficult this is."

Relenting, he took her hand again and patted it. He liked being able to reassure her, she noted dully. He enjoyed feeling magnanimous. "I understand," he said. "Naturally you don't wish to be parted. Nor do I! We must write to each other during the separation. That will make it easier. Before you know it, the two years will have passed, and we shall be together again."

Tears gathered in her eyes, of frustration as much as sorrow. "Freddie, I beg you, can you not make some arrangement for me with your family? Are you so certain they won't permit any kind of engagement?"

He pressed his lips to her hand, but his eyes were already seeking an exit; he was eager to end this uncomfortable conversation. "It is quite impossible, I fear. Now, be of good courage. I shall write to you soon."

Then, unbelievably, he was gone. She sat down hard on the spindly gilded chair that was all the furniture the alcove afforded.

The *idiot*.

Did he truly think she would wait for him—that she *could* wait, even if she wanted to?

In agitation she bit her thumbnail through her glove, a habit she had not been able to break, and caught the unpleasant smell of the spirits of turpentine with which she had cleaned the kid leather the night before. Since she could not afford new gloves she had to extend the life of these as long as possible, even though she loathed the smell and feared that her dancing partners were aware of it.

She tried to think, but her thoughts flapped about like birds startled into flight. It was already too late to find another beau. The Season was too near its end; to fix her sights on another man would only make everyone believe she was a shallow creature unworthy of a good man's love. Worse, since everyone knew that she and Freddie had had an unofficial understanding, there would now be suspicion about her innocence. Other potential suitors—and certainly their wary parents—would wonder whether she was soiled goods. Even if they did not suspect her virtue, they would wonder what flaw was great enough to result in the sudden breaking off of so seemingly solid an attachment. Freddie had wrecked her chances for this Season.

She must find Cousin Margaret and confer with her. Perhaps there was a solution Cecily had not thought of.

But she hesitated to leave the shelter of the alcove. Her pride rebelled at being seen by anyone in her state of distress. She could picture all too clearly the looks of curiosity and speculation if she appeared alone in the midst of the other couples.

If she could make her way unnoticed to the ladies' cloakroom, she might escape the humiliation of stares and whispers. Perhaps she could have the attendant smuggle a note to her cousin.

She rose and peeped out of the alcove. Across the hall the double doors were open to the ballroom, and the noise and music that poured out gave her a pang of sadness. She loved to dance the waltz, and this one—which she had promised to Freddie—was proceeding without her.

As inconspicuously as she could, holding her hands against her taffeta skirts to prevent them from rustling, she crept down the hall toward the ladies' cloakroom.

"Miss Jaine!"

It was a man's voice that halted her. Reluctantly, she turned to meet the unexpected sight of Mr. Connor Blake.

Unexpected, but not altogether unwelcome. Mr. Blake was the subject of much fascination among Cecily's fellow debutantes. Widowed little more than a year ago after a tragically brief marriage, he had the pensive air and soulful dark eyes of a man still mourning his loss, but as a man of

less than forty years of age with a still youthful face and figure, he was believed to be not yet past hope of remarriage.
Cecily had found his aloofness intriguing, for he attended
many balls but never danced, preferring to be an onlooker—
perhaps absorbed in the bittersweet pleasure of reminisc-
ing about his late wife. His grave courtesy and faraway gaze
exerted endless fascination for Cousin Margaret, who liked
to call him Byronic.

So Cecily felt an honor was being conferred upon her
when he approached her. "Miss Jaine," he repeated, "I hope
you are not leaving us so soon."

"I—I fear I must."

"Is there any way in which I can assist you?" From the
courteous concern in his eyes, Cecily could not be certain
whether he had observed what had happened and was
simply too polite to mention it. Up close, the velvety dark
eyes were all the more compelling, and his voice beautifully
resonant. He was no taller than Freddie, and lacked Freddie's golden hair and crystalline blue eyes, but something
about him gave a sense of steadiness, of security, as though
there would be no safer place on earth than in his arms.

Such fancies! She gathered her straying thoughts. "It's
very kind of you, Mr. Blake—"

"Not at all, Miss Jaine. I am honored to put myself at
your disposal."

"Well, if you would not mind letting my cousin know
that I am ready to depart," she said, "that would be most
helpful."

He did not respond at once, though his eyes never left
her face. The tenderness of his gaze would be her undoing;
she tried to master the tears that rose to her eyes. Then her
hand was in his, and he was closing her fingers around his
handkerchief.

"If you are determined to go, of course I shall not stop you," he said softly. "But, if you will forgive my frankness, young Mr. Hightower's behavior, disgraceful though it was, should not prevent you from enjoying the evening."

Oh, horrors. "You heard?"

"I heard little enough, but I know something of the Hightower family's disposition—enough to guess what may have left you in such distress." His voice was low and sympathetic. "Miss Jaine, if you will permit a bit of advice from an elder, please trust that your heart will heal. You will not forget your sorrow, but you can learn to live with it, even to forget it from time to time."

A heated protest rose to her lips, but she remembered in time that this man knew heartbreak himself, even though the circumstances were different. And he meant to be kind. Indeed, it was soothing to listen to the low murmur of his voice. Her hand still lay in his, and she made no motion to free it.

"Thank you," she said. "I am grateful for your kindness."

"I've done nothing worth your thanks, unless you will consent to let me have my carriage brought around for you and your cousin." He paused. "Perhaps, though, you might give me a waltz before you depart?"

"Well..." It would be rather satisfying to go dancing past Freddie in the arms of another man—a wealthy man at that, a catch. Her pride warred with her wish to vanish from the eyes of the world and nurse her bruised heart in private.

He seemed to sense her struggle, for he smiled. It was the first time she had seen him do so, and the transformation in him was breathtaking: handsome before, he now seemed younger, full of warmth and humor. "It will give the gossips something else to talk about besides Mr. Hightower no longer being by your side," he said.

How wise he was! It must come with his age and experience. Her heart swelled with gratitude and a kind of wondering pleasure that he should single her out for his help.

"I didn't think you ever danced," she could not help saying. "All this Season, I never saw you on the floor."

"Not since my wife's death," he allowed, his eyes far away. "But somehow I think I should enjoy it tonight—if you will do me the honor."

How much he must have adored his wife—and how flattered Cecily was to be the woman to finally bring him out of his self-imposed exile from pleasure. She smiled and straightened, using his handkerchief to blot away the last vestiges of tears. "I should be delighted, Mr. Blake," she said.

When she entered the ballroom on his arm, the last song was just concluding. Suddenly everyone was looking at them. Across the room, Freddie stood with his mother, both staring at her and her escort with satisfyingly shocked faces. *Did you expect me to sit weeping in that alcove for the rest of the night?* she thought. Desirable a match though he might be, Freddie needed to learn that she would not spend her life waiting on him. Cousin Margaret, too, was staring, and Cecily gave her a reassuring smile.

It was pleasant indeed to be the object of everyone's attention—for the right reasons—as the orchestra struck up the next tune and Mr. Blake took her in his arms. No one watching her would think that her heart had been broken or that Freddie Hightower had ruined her life.

Then, as Mr. Blake led her into the dance, his eyes intent upon her face as his hand on her back guided her, she felt a fluttering beneath her ribs that spoke of something new. This was more than gratitude for helping her save face. More than the satisfaction of dealing a slap to her erstwhile suitor.

Perhaps Freddie had actually done her a favor—and given her the chance to know a finer man.

In astonishingly short order, he brought up marriage.

Cecily could scarcely believe at first what Mr. Blake was asking. "You wish me to be your wife?" she said. "But we've known each other for such a short time."

Even as she spoke the words she was mentally scolding herself. *Idiot girl! This is your chance—your way out of poverty and into a life of security. What does it matter if you and he are all but strangers to each other? He is wealthy, respectable, and kind. That is all you need know.*

It was five days after the ball, and they were having tea in the parlor of a genteel hotel. Mr. Blake, having arrived at the down-at-heel lodgings where Cecily and Cousin Margaret were staying, took one look at the shabby parlor and announced that they would be his guests that day. Cecily's face still burned with embarrassment as she remembered the look on his face when he had seen the seediness in which she lived. Before now they had met in public gardens and the like, but today, all it took was a glance around at the mended, mismatched furnishings, the stained and faded wallpaper—and no doubt one whiff of the permanent smells of cooked cabbage and tallow candles—and he had viewed her in a new light.

But Mr. Blake had not seemed to hold it against her—had actually, in fact, seemed to become more tender, more solicitous.

And now this. A proposal. It was scarcely possible.

Yet here he was, taking her hand in his and speaking softly to her, so that Cousin Margaret, tactfully loitering across the room ostensibly examining a painting, would not hear.

"I completely understand your hesitation," he said. "You hadn't an idea I was in the world until less than a week ago, and now I am asking you to pledge yourself to me for life."

Well, that was scarcely accurate. She had certainly been aware of him as an interesting and attractive enigma, but she need not tell him that. She tried to brush away such irrelevant thoughts and pay attention as he continued to speak.

"With that in mind, if you and your worthy cousin would like to be certain of my finances, you may call on my banker to discuss the subject with him."

"Good heavens, of course not," she exclaimed. "I'd never dream of such a thing, Mr. Blake." She did not mention that she and Cousin Margaret had already been making discreet inquiries about his financial status and had been satisfied by all the reports on him. "Your reputation as an upstanding gentleman is all the assurance I need," she said.

His smile was touched with melancholy, and she felt it stir something in her. His dark eyes were very tender.

"I expected you would say such a thing," he murmured, and the intimate tone of his voice was like a caress. "You are so good and so innocent that you have no idea what dissemblers men can be. Had you a parent to look after your welfare, I'd not need to trouble you with such sordid matters. As it is, I shall speak to your cousin about these practicalities—and spend my time with you discoursing on more pleasant subjects."

He was clearly happy to take the conversation in a more loverlike direction, but as much as she would have enjoyed that, she knew she needed to be honest with him while he still had a chance to reverse course. Never let it be said that she had trapped him into marriage.

"I appreciate your being so honest with me, Mr. Blake," she said, "and I owe it to you to do so in return. You have probably guessed that my cousin and I are... poor." The word did not want to be spoken; it lodged in her throat, and she had to force it out. "I cannot in good faith allow you to assume that we are living beneath our means. The fact is that my parents died when I was quite young, and Cousin Margaret is my only family. She is a spinster with only a small income. We have not had an easy life, I must confess. The existence you offer me as your wife sounds like a beautiful dream, and I long to accept it. But," she added as he made to speak, "I cannot do so under false pretenses. It is important that you know that I bring nothing—*nothing*—to this marriage. I shall understand completely if you wish to let the matter drop, and I promise I shall not force you to go through with an engagement you may find disadvantageous."

It was quite the longest speech she had ever made to him, having heretofore mostly let him do the talking, as she knew men liked to do, and he took his time in replying. Waiting, she heard the beating of her heart in her ears and wondered if she had just thrown away her last chance at happiness.

"Miss Jaine," he said at last, and took her other hand in his. "Your honesty and courage do you credit. Rest assured that I have made no false guarantees to myself about any wealth you would bring to the marriage. But you are gravely mistaken when you say you bring nothing. Your dear and adorable self is all that I desire, and indeed I look forward to gratifying your every wish so that in time the memory of the straitened circumstances of your past will grow fainter and fainter until it vanishes altogether."

She felt almost lightheaded with relief and happiness. It was really happening. She would never again need to worry about where her next meal was coming from or if she and her cousin would be evicted for failing to pay their rent.

"In that case, Mr. Blake," she said, "I am honored to accept your proposal."

Such pleasure leapt into his eyes then that she felt awed. It was true, then: he truly wanted her. Bowing his head, he kissed first her right hand, then her left. In so public a place it did not go unnoticed, and an interested murmur reached her ears. But she was too happy to care.

The murmur rippled over to Cousin Margaret, who materialized at the table in her function as chaperone. "Is everything all right, my dear?"

Mr. Blake rose from his chair and took her hand. "My dear Cousin Margaret—may I call you that?—you are just in time to drink a toast with us. Your cousin has graciously consented to be mine."

Margaret's pale eyes sought Cecily's for confirmation, and Cecily hastened to reassure her. "Mr. Blake and I have become engaged," she said.

"My goodness! Why, how lovely. What an exciting development," she fluttered, as Mr. Blake held a chair for her and beckoned to a waiter. "When shall the ceremony be?"

"As soon as possible. And in the meantime I must insist that both of you leave your current lodgings and take rooms here. I shall arrange everything, of course—you needn't worry about the details."

Cecily thought of a servant from this fashionable establishment retrieving her meager belongings, no doubt with a sneer at their shabbiness, then decided not to think about it. "Where shall we have the wedding breakfast?"

He flashed a dazzling smile at her. Gone was the brooding widower; her husband-to-be was now revealed to be a charming, lively man with an unexpected dimple. "We'll have it here at the hotel," he said. "No doubt they can even recommend a seamstress to complete a trousseau for you in no time. Where would you like to honeymoon, my dear? Rome? Lucerne? Both?"

He truly did mean to pamper her, to treat her like a princess. Suddenly she felt like crying out of sheer gratitude. He had truly rescued her when she seemed to have lost everything.

"Whatever you prefer," she said, and though she could not find words to express all that she felt, from the way his glance lingered on her she thought he knew what she meant.

The murmur around them swelled into a lively rumble when Mr. Blake directed the waiters to take wine to all of the tables so that everyone might toast to their happiness. In a daze she raised her own glass, glancing around to see people beaming at them. "To my bride to be!" Mr. Blake exclaimed, raising his glass high, and the toast was echoed loudly.

Cecily drank, and the wine bubbled and tingled against her palate. No longer would she be forced to use tea leaves over and over until she was drinking only hot water. No more stale bread and runny stew. No more nights when she could not fall asleep because of her icy feet and empty belly.

Then she heard the voice from behind her. Not meant for her ears, pitched low, but nonetheless quite clear amid the hubbub of good cheer.

"Let us hope she fares better than the first wife," said the voice. "If the rumors are true, Eleanor Blake came to a tragic end."

She looked around, but she could find no clear culprit. Then she felt a touch on her arm and found Mr. Blake—her fiancé, as she must learn to think of him—standing very close to her. The very presence of him was reassuring; his height and the breadth of his shoulders gave him a solidity that made her feel protected.

"Anything amiss, my dear?"

"No, nothing," she said. She found a smile for him, which was not difficult. She was practiced at making herself pleasant. "Nothing at all. I'm entirely happy."

His gaze was searching, as though he suspected this was not the whole truth, but when she said nothing further he relaxed. "As am I, thanks to you," he said.

She marveled at it. She was all that he wanted; she made him happy. Without money or distinguished connections or social cachet. It was both humbling and thrilling.

When the thought of Freddie Hightower did finally find its way into her mind, it brought a tiny pang, to be sure, but then disdain swept all sentimental considerations away.

If he had been half the man Mr. Blake was, he might have been the one claiming her now—but even so, would she have been happy with a man so easily led away from her, so indecisive, so callow?

No. She had only fancied she loved Freddie. Connor Blake was the man who would make her life a contented one.

CHAPTER TWO
Eleanor (1858)

When Eleanor was summoned to the building site, she was just tying off the bandage on old Mrs. Suthern's sprained wrist. The old lady was inclined to be talkative, and Eleanor was grateful for the reprieve. When she emerged from the dimness of the house the sunlight made her blink. The July air was crystalline, and she breathed it in gratefully as she crossed the road and crested the slight rise toward the site where the new hospital was slowly taking form.

"Ah, there she is! Eleanor, my dear, over here." Her father beckoned her over to where he stood beside a man in shirtsleeves whose left hand, as she could tell even at this distance, was bleeding profusely. "She'll soon set you to rights," her father continued, his voice as benign as his white-whiskered face, and he clapped the wounded man on the shoulder.

"I shall certainly do my best," she said, but her mind was buzzing with questions now that she was near enough to get a proper look at the bleeding man. His face was less ruddy and weathered than those of his companions, as if he had not been long in this line of work. His clothing, too, was not that of a laborer; his boots were well polished, his shirt of fine linen. His waving dark hair had been barbered, and not long ago. Despite the fashion for beards, he was clean shaven.

15

Her father's voice broke into her observations. "My dear, this is Second Lieutenant Connor Blake—or is it just Lieutenant?"

"I no longer use my military rank, sir." His low, rich voice fell pleasantly on her ear, without the harsh accent she had anticipated.

"Very well then, Mr. Blake. Allow me to introduce my daughter, Eleanor."

She greeted the man with a brief nod, less comfortable with social niceties than with injuries. To her surprise, he responded to her perfunctory greeting with a graceful bow.

"I must throw myself upon your mercy, Miss Fairley," he said. "Or else my own clumsiness will prevent me from being any real good to your father's hospital."

"Nonsense, nonsense," Mr. Fairley exclaimed. "You didn't survive some of the most brutal fighting in the Crimea only to fall a cripple here in Surrey! Well, I shall leave you in my daughter's capable hands. Let me know if you need me to send someone for Dr. Carmody, my dear."

Her father, though courageous in most ways, was averse to the sight of blood, and he left them without a backward glance.

"How did your injury happen?" she asked, her interest piqued by the mention of the Crimea. She indicated for the injured man to take a seat on a low stone coping and fished some cotton wool out of her medical bag. When she held out her hand he obligingly placed his wounded hand in hers, and she began to blot the blood away so that she could see how badly he was hurt.

"It was an idiotic thing to do," he said. He had a handsome voice, she thought; it would have made him a success in the theater, and listening to him speak made her wonder why a man with his gifts and bearing had chosen a career that rewarded physical strength above all else. The hand

she held was fine-boned and aristocratic, with few cal-
louses.

"Idiotic in what way?" she asked.

His rueful smile seemed to include her in a secret just
between them, and the intimacy of it sent a tendril of pleasure through her breast. "I was impatient to scrape off a
stray bit of mortar, and rather than taking the time to seek
out the proper tool, I used my penknife. It slipped, not surprisingly, and now—well, you see the result."

"That's unfortunate." The gash at the base of his left
thumb was ugly, but the edges were clean enough that they
should knit well. She sat down next to him and drew a
curved needle and silk thread from her bag. "I'm afraid I
shall have to stitch it up," she said. "I've whiskey in my bag
if you would like something to dull the pain."

"No, thank you."

"You needn't abstain for fear of losing face," she said,
having encountered this misguided stoicism in men before.
"I'd much rather you not faint while I'm about my work."

To her surprise, rather than sputtering in affronted dignity he smiled. "Just talk to me," he said. "That will be
pleasant enough distraction from your activities."

"But what shall I talk to you about?"

"For a start, tell me how you came to be so capable at
stitching up wounds. Were you with Miss Nightingale in the
war?"

She bent her head over her work so that he would not
see regret or resentment in her face. "I wanted to go," she
said. "I trained for it. But Papa didn't wish for me to."

That mild summation barely hinted at the reality. The
pleading and cajoling on both sides, the tears—again on
both sides. Bluster from her father, who never blustered.
And at last her own capitulation when she realized that he
would be completely alone not only for the duration of the

war but perhaps even permanently if anything should prevent her return. The field hospitals were rife with disease, and she could not assure him with certainty that she would escape it.

And her heart misgave her when she imagined leaving him to that loneliness, whether it was for a year or far longer. They had been all the family each other had for many years now, and she feared he would have been lost without her.

All the same, she had had to fight against bitterness. Her life here in England felt so empty of purpose, and she had longed for the chance to do something more than manage a household and look after her father, dear though he was.

A hiss of indrawn breath reminded her that she needed to distract her patient from her work. "At least I can offer our neighbors some care," she said brightly. "How did you fare? Were you wounded in the fighting?"

"Not to speak of—nothing like some of my comrades, certainly. I was lucky to return home at all, to take up the life that really engages me."

Surely he did not mean constructing buildings. Then she thought she understood.

"Architecture?" she guessed, and his quick smile almost made her forget what she was doing. He had a handsomely formed mouth and chin and a strong profile that made her think of classical statuary. His hooded dark eyes were intent, even piercing. An unforgettable face.

"Exactly," he said, bringing her wandering thoughts back to the conversation. "My studies have been only haphazard, due to my other commitments..."

Commitments such as a wife? The thought popped into her head before she could guard against it, and she tried to dismiss it as the foolishness it was.

"...so I leaped at the opportunity to work with the distinguished Lemuel Fairley." He watched as she wrapped a clean bandage around her stitching. "I did not realize that the great architect would have an equally brilliant daughter."

The flattery pleased her more than it should have, and she made herself take it as a joke. "No one has ever accused me of being brilliant, Mr. Blake," she said as she secured the end of the bandage. "I have acquired some useful skills, but in all other respects I am perfectly ordinary."

Before she knew what he intended, his bandaged hand had moved to clasp hers, and he drew her closer. She found herself gazing into dark eyes that held such purpose and conviction that her own will seemed to flicker and die.

Softly he said, "You sell yourself short, Miss Fairley. Not only do you stitch up my wound with such skill, but you make the pain of it disappear in the sweetness of your company."

Eleanor was not accustomed to being struck speechless, but she could find no words fit for a response as the man's magnetic gaze held hers. She was full thirty years of age and no beauty, and after a tepid romance at age nineteen had entertained few suitors despite her father's wealth. Compliments of this sort, and spoken in so compelling a murmur, were simply not part of her life.

With an effort of will she drew back, freeing her hand. She realized the other workers were watching them, and she had no desire to look foolish before them.

"Your wound should heal without difficulty if you can keep it clean and avoid using that hand," she said briskly. "Come to me in ten days or so, and I shall be glad to remove the stitches."

Grimacing, he regarded his wound. "It will take some ingenuity to work single-handed," he said. "This is the kind of labor that one needs to be sound of body to carry out."

It occurred to her that this job of work might be vital to keeping him fed and sheltered. Even this minor injury might prove a serious impediment to his earning a living.

"I shall speak to my father," she said. "I'm sure he'll find a solution. Pray excuse me."

She was almost glad of the pretext to leave his presence for a few minutes. Never before had she met a man who made her feel so scattered and witless—and yet it was not as disagreeable as sensation as she would have expected. She had to fight the impulse to look back over her shoulder to see if he was watching her.

Her father was not far off, observing work on the foundations. He looked thoughtful at what she had to say, then brightened.

"Invite the lad to dine with us tonight," he said. "We can talk about his future and see that he gets at least one decent meal."

Privately Eleanor thought that "lad" was a peculiar way to refer to someone as impressive as Connor Blake, but her father, who as a man would be impervious to such things, had probably not observed the younger man's magnetism and strength of bearing. When she looked around for Mr. Blake she was startled to find him watching her, standing quite still. With her heart beating a little bit more quickly than usual she approached.

"My father bids you join us for our evening meal," she said.

"And you?"

"Well—I join in the invitation, of course."

"Then I am pleased to accept."

Holding his gaze was making her flustered again, so she drew out her card. "Here is our address. We are on Bridewell Lane. You needn't dress," she added, and immediately realized that might have sounded as if it were a concession, which might prick his pride. "Papa and I rarely do," she said quickly.

There was a trace of amusement in his dark eyes, as though he suspected she was merely covering for her gaffe. "I look forward to this evening all the same," he said, "even without the enticement of seeing you in evening dress."

She must put an end to this. "Mr. Blake, I enjoy compliments as much as the next young woman, but—"

"Do you?"

The interruption put her off balance. "Do I what?"

"Enjoy compliments." Now she was certain of the amusement in his gaze. "I fear I may have unintentionally caused you embarrassment, which is the last thing I should wish to do."

Thank goodness he was perceptive enough that she would not have to say it herself. "It is just that there is a time and a place for such things. And we are practically strangers. When you say such flattering things, I—I simply don't know where to look."

The smile that curved his lips was somehow intimate; it suggested that the two of them were bound together in some private way by this conversation. "Then look at me," he said.

As if I could look at anything else, she thought, feeling the heat of a blush in her cheeks. "Six o'clock," she said, aware that her voice was breathless, and hastened away to her father with the distinct sensation that all the laborers were watching her and observing her flustered state.

He was prompt to arrive at dinner, dressed in a worn but well-cut suit that was damp at the shoulders where he had walked through the rain. Eleanor immediately reproached herself for not having offered to send a carriage for him; no doubt he was lodging in a rooming house near the building site. She noticed that his suit was a trifle large even on his strong frame. Perhaps he had been ill; so many soldiers returning from the Crimea had been wasted by sickness. And if he had left the army, which seemed to be the case, he might not have been able to afford regular meals. She was glad she had instructed the cook to prepare a couple of extra dishes to make the meal more hearty.

Mr. Blake proved to be entertaining company. At her father's request, he related thrilling stories of the fighting in the Crimea, adding little human touches about his comrades in arms that awakened Eleanor's interest and sympathy. All went well until the plates from the soup course were removed, when he looked with some chagrin at the chops that George, the footman, brought in for the main course.

"I fear I may be quite clumsy with knife and fork," he said, indicating his bandaged hand with a wry smile. "I am under the orders of a very charming nurse to use my hand as little as possible."

"Oh, Eleanor will help you," her father said promptly— so promptly, indeed, that she narrowed a look at him. But his expression was guileless, so she drew a chair up to Mr. Blake's side, feeling those penetrating dark eyes resting on her as she cut up his chop. "Still, I'm sure it's nothing to what you got in the war," her father continued. "Come now, you must have stories of your own to share. You've told us a great deal about the bravery of your comrades, but not of your own exploits."

Mr. Blake shrugged, and she caught the masculine scents of bay rum and leather. "There's little enough to tell. I always thought the medal was far too generous."

"You were awarded a medal?" Eleanor exclaimed.

"It isn't as grand as it sounds. It just happened that during a charge the standard bearer for my regiment went down, shot in the head, poor bloke. It seemed to me that someone ought to take up the colors. As I went to retrieve them I took a bullet in one leg, but I still managed to seize the banner and limp along with it in some fashion." He grimaced. "I'm told I passed out eventually, but the next thing I remember was waking up in the field hospital."

"And your leg?" Eleanor asked. "Was the wound serious?" She didn't recall seeing him limp.

"Not very. The bullet missed the bone and passed straight through. I was lucky—luckier than the poor devils around me fighting infection and disease." He smiled at Eleanor, his dark eyes warming, and for a second she forgot to breathe. "We needed more nurses like you," he said.

She did not answer but concentrated on his plate. The marrows were slightly undercooked and needed cutting.

"To leave all that behind to study architecture is quite a change," her father said. "How did that come about?"

Mr. Blake did not answer immediately, and when she raised her head to see if anything was amiss she was startled at his nearness. His face was so close to hers that she could feel the warmth of his skin. For a moment he just looked into her eyes.

"Architecture," he repeated. Then he cleared his throat, breaking the stare, and spoke with more confidence. "The fighting changed me," he said to her father. "When I returned I found I could not return to my old life. I needed to understand what exactly I was fighting to defend—what works of man are worth killing for. So I left the army and resolved to spend some time simply taking those opportunities that were offered and trying to determine what I could feel passionate about. I traveled, met new people, encountered different ways of living."

"How exciting," Eleanor said, taken with the idea. "What adventures you must have had. Though nothing, I'm sure, equal to your time in combat."

"It has been illuminating," he said, and his voice dropped into a tone meant especially for her. "But not truly exciting until now."

Eleanor, having finished her task, rose to return to her place at the table. She did not dare look at her father in case he saw too much in her face. He seemed not to have heard their guest's low words. But then, he was growing a bit deaf. "And so during this peripatetic existence you realized that you wanted to become an architect," he said.

"Yes, sir," Mr. Blake said, in a normal tone of voice once more. "Of course, as a man of five-and-thirty I know it's late in life for me to take up such a course of study—"

"Nonsense, lad. In any case, with me to teach you and introduce you to all the best minds in the business, you'll soon make up for any lost time. There's no need for you to continue as a laborer." He shook his fork at the guest with mock sternness. "No more penknife injuries for you, my boy!"

Mr. Blake smiled. "Sir, I can hardly complain about my mischance when it served to introduce me to you and your beautiful daughter."

"Fiddlesticks," Eleanor muttered, embarrassed but pleased. She was perfectly ordinary looking, with her brown hair and gray eyes. The only beautiful feature she might have possessed was her complexion, which old ladies sometimes exclaimed over. Mr. Blake probably thought he could win her father over by complimenting her.

Except that her father had not been present for the compliments he had paid her at the building site, which scotched that theory.

"Do you have any other family close by?" their guest was asking now.

She shook her head. "My mother and my little brother succumbed to a fever many years ago. Papa and I have only each other." She smiled at her father across the table, and he leaned over to pat her hand.

"And no man could ask for a better daughter to look after him," he said, beaming. "I'm the last male child of my line, Mr. Blake, though at least Eleanor was able to know her grandfather before he passed." He chuckled and added slyly, "Not that she was overfond of him."

At an inquiring look from Mr. Blake, she said, "My grandfather found it amusing to frighten me. Whenever we visited him at his estate on the Norfolk coast, Sterne House, he would torment me with ghost stories and gruesome tales of the wreckers who used to set false lights to lure unwary ships. He claimed that the house was riddled with secret passages and hidden chambers that the wreckers used to hide themselves and their loot."

"Riddled with ghosts as well," her father reminded her. "There was the lady in white with only three fingers on each hand, the rest having been cut off by looters eager for her rings."

"How could I ever forget her?" Eleanor's shudder was only half assumed. "As a child I could hardly sleep for keeping watch—I was certain that in the night a hidden door would creak open and admit a ghost, or a wrecker, or the ghost of a wrecker." No, she did not miss her grandfather or visits to his dreary house. She had no idea how such a malicious old sinner had produced a son as kind and jovial as her father, but the contrast had made her appreciate her father all the more.

"Come to think of it," Mr. Blake said, "I believe I have heard stories of wreckers operating off the coast of Norfolk."

"Sterne House occupies a treacherous bit of coastline," Mr. Fairley said. "The sands beneath the waters are restless, always shifting. You need not look to wreckers to explain ships foundering there."

"Perhaps Grandfather thought wreckers made a more romantic story," said Eleanor. "Or perhaps he just liked to frighten me. In any case, after his death we had the place closed up."

"Indeed," her father said. "I'm considering having the roof removed so we'll no longer have to pay taxes on the old pile; it's scarcely fit to live in."

"My father's only joking," Eleanor explained when their guest raised his eyebrows. "The taxes aren't a burden, but the house may not be safe for habitation anymore. Papa is more concerned about some trespasser tumbling through a rotted staircase or being struck by falling masonry."

"I should think you'd want to preserve it," Mr. Blake said. "How long has Sterne House been in your family?"

"Oh, centuries. It started life as a castle and is said to have been a Royalist safe house during the Civil War." But Mr. Fairley's attention was wandering back to his favorite topic, and the conversation turned back to architecture for the remainder of the meal.

Eleanor was secretly grateful that she could merely listen and observe their guest. He had little to do himself but listen, as Mr. Fairley could expound upon his favorite subject for hours together. She observed in some surprise that, while Mr. Blake's features were so strong as to appear almost harsh in repose, when animated there was a sensitivity to his eyes and mouth that gave him an entirely different appearance.

Occasionally his gaze would turn her way, and when his eyes chanced to meet hers she gave him an apologetic look for her father's garrulous tendency. But he did not look bored or impatient, and she felt a rush of gratitude toward him on her father's behalf.

As soon as she could find an opening in her father's discourse she excused herself and left them to their port. Settling in the parlor with some gauze bandages to roll, she could still hear their voices, her father's going on at length, Mr. Blake's inserting the odd question or comment that sent the older man off in full flood again. It was a companionable sort of music, and she smiled to hear them getting along so well.

When they finally emerged to join her, her father's blue eyes were bright with enthusiasm as he clapped their guest on the shoulder. Seeing them standing side by side made her realize just how tall and well set-up Mr. Blake was by contrast. He was an impressive figure, no doubt about it. She remembered that he had never clarified whether the commitments he spoke of included a wife or children.

Now he came to join her on the divan and reached out, raising an inquiring eyebrow, to touch her work. "Miss Fairley," he said, "I should imagine that most young ladies of your station would be found sewing a fine seam of an evening. Yet you have found something more constructive to do."

"Though she did hanker to go off to the war, Eleanor has found plenty of use for her knowledge without leaving her home country," her father announced. Port had made him expansive, and his face was ruddy around his white whiskers. "And surely you, Mr. Blake, can find the same! With your sharp intellect and drive, England needs more men like you at home. And still so young, even after all of your exploits in the army!" He sighed. "I wish I were younger. My daughter is a capable young woman, as you can tell, but I can't bear to think of her alone after I pass beyond the veil."

Good heavens, how much port had he drunk, to discuss such personal things? She cast about for a safer topic.

But her father's words seemed to have alarmed their visitor—or insulted him—for instead of taking a seat he said, "I fear I have taken up too much of your time already. As much as I have enjoyed this evening—and I can't thank you enough for inviting me into your home—it's time I was on my way."

"It's early yet," Mr. Fairley protested. "Eleanor, induce him to stay."

"Please don't rush off," she said, but Mr. Blake smiled and shook his head.

"Work on the hospital starts early in the morning," he said. "If I'm late, the other men will never let me forget it."

Mr. Fairley looked as though he wanted to protest, but instead he capitulated. "Well, I can hardly fault you for being responsible," he said. Eleanor rang for Alice, the parlormaid, to bring their guest's hat and gloves.

"You must come again," she said to him, not certain whether she truly hoped he would. She was unused to men who awoke such turbulent and confused emotions in her.

"Nothing would please me better." Mr. Blake shook her father's hand and bowed low over hers, and then, straightening, went quite still. He looked long at the room, and

Eleanor could have sworn he was trying to commit it to memory.

"I can't say how much tonight has meant to me," he said. His gaze dwelled on the cozy room with the family portraits, old-fashioned fire screen, and plump cushioned armchairs, and then on Mr. Fairley and Eleanor themselves. "I wish I had known you before the war. If I had been able to take this picture with me into battle, it might have strengthened me, given me an ideal to hold in my heart."

"But surely you had your own home in mind," Eleanor began, but he shook his head.

"Mine never looked so peaceful or tranquil. I'd have liked to have a memory of the beauty I see before me now."

This last he spoke to Eleanor, and she had a startled moment of wondering whether he meant that to refer to her rather than her home. Perhaps he guessed this, for he added in a low voice as she walked with him to the door, "If I have been perhaps too forward tonight, too eager to make you like me, I hope you will do me the courtesy of attributing it to my delight at experiencing such a home as yours. Being here with you and your father made me feel quite poignantly the contrast with my own home." He grimaced. "I was a younger son, you see, and my elder brother outshone me terribly. My father...well, suffice it to say that he was a far cry from yours."

"I'm sorry to hear it." Before she could think better of it, she added on impulse, "You must consider us to be your family while you are in town. I can tell my father is eager to take you under his wing, since he has no son of his own."

"What a delightful idea. I should love to claim you as family." The way he looked at her made her self-conscious suddenly. It was not a brotherly sort of look. But all he said was "Thank you for tonight, Miss Fairley."

When he had descended the front steps and the maid had shut the door behind him, Eleanor returned to the parlor, deep in thought, to find her father warming himself by the fire.

"I like him," he announced, making Eleanor laugh.

"So I saw," she said. "Well, I think I like him as well." *Like.* Such an insipid word for such a strong and complicated deluge of emotions.

She continued to warm to Mr. Blake the more she saw of him. Mr. Fairley insisted on having him to dinner every day, and she quickly grew accustomed to hearing the sound of their voices in genial conversation in her father's study. Nor did Mr. Blake fail to spend time conversing with her as well, inquiring after the well-being of her "patients" and inviting her out for the occasional walk in the park so that, he said, her own health would not suffer neglect from being shut inside too much. He seemed to notice how uncomfortable compliments made her, for he restrained himself from flattering her as much as he had that first evening. She was touched by this, especially when he caught himself up and she could tell that he was exercising restraint. The compliments he did not pay almost meant more than the ones he did.

All the same, it startled her when she learned just how much her father had come to esteem their new friend. One day after their midday meal he said abruptly, "I haven't liked to say anything to you, Eleanor, but I worry about what will happen to you when I'm gone. You'll have money enough and to spare, but who shall keep you company? Whom will you rely on for comfort and protection? It distresses me to think of your being lonely."

"Hush, Papa. No one could replace you."

He wasn't listening. "But a fine upstanding young man like Mr. Blake, a war hero, a man who actively contemplates what use to put his life to and what legacy he will leave—that is a man I could trust to look after you."

This was the first time he had ever tried to play matchmaker for her, and she wasn't certain she liked it. "I'm old enough not to need looking after," she pointed out, sidestepping the topic of Mr. Blake, but her father reached for her hand and squeezed it as if he felt she needed consoling.

"Your age need not be an insurmountable barrier," he said. "I've seen the way he looks at you every night." As she was too taken aback to respond, he rushed on. "Promise me, my dear, that when I'm gone you will think about what I've said."

"Papa, it hardly seems—"

"Please, Eleanor." His white-whiskered face was unusually earnest, his eyes beseeching, and she realized that he truly was concerned for her.

"I promise," she said.

She said it merely to humor him, never dreaming that in just a short time she would be forced to contemplate his wishes for her. For, within a fortnight, Eleanor's father was dead.

CHAPTER THREE
Cecily

News of the engagement spread swiftly, and Cecily found herself invited to dinners and parties with her fiancé. Every other waking hour was busy as well—being fitted for new clothes, including her wedding gown; writing invitations to the wedding breakfast (though she had few acquaintances to invite); and going shopping for all that she would need for their wedding tour.

There was Cousin Margaret to settle, as well. Mr. Blake—Connor—had drawn her out until she had finally admitted a secret desire to settle near an old friend in Blackpool, and in short order he had secured a comfortable cottage for her and settled an amount of money on her that would allow her to live respectably for the rest of her days.

"Though of course I shall miss you dreadfully, dear Cecily," she said. But her gaze was dreamy, as if she was already envisioning a future of tending a tiny garden and walking to church with her friend, and Cecily realized that both would be a tiny bit relieved to be parting. Their personalities were dissimilar, and Cousin Margaret had found society to be exhausting, along with the constant effort to ingratiate themselves with acquaintances who could take them in for weeks or months. Cecily herself was delighted that her meals and lodgings would never again be dependent upon her own charm and wit, so she could only imagine how relieved her cousin must be to end this uncertain way of living.

Only one incident marred this happy time. Out shopping one day, she was turning over brooches in a display tray, waiting for Connor to rejoin her, when there came a choked whisper of "Cecily!"

She looked up to find Freddie Hightower standing before her, He did not look well. There were shadows beneath his eyes, and his usually immaculate hair was rumpled, as though he no longer cared about his appearance. His earnest blue eyes were fixed on her with an expression that would have softened her heart if she had let it. But she would not let it.

"Oh, hello," she said offhandedly. "Fancy seeing you here." She was pleasantly conscious of being well turned-out in a new bonnet and wished that she had a pretext to remove her glove and reveal the large emerald engagement ring she wore.

"I came to have my watch repaired," he said. "Are you— is your—"

"We are here to confer with the jeweler, and my fiancé shall return very soon." She took a mean pleasure when he winced at her use of the term. Served him right.

Then, to her astonishment, he reached for her hand. "I must speak with you," he said, his words hushed but rapid with urgency. "I was a fool. You were right, and I should have stood up to my parents."

"Indeed? Do you mean that you're ready to defy them now and marry me?"

His gaze wavered. "I don't know. But there must be some way to make them come round. Can we meet somewhere to talk?"

This was the limit. How dare he try to woo her back now that she had security, when he still had none to offer? It was outrageous.

"No, we cannot," she snapped. "As far as I am concerned, we have nothing to say to each other." At that moment Connor appeared in the doorway to the back of the shop, and she pitched her voice to meet his ears. "Please release my hand, Mr. Hightower."

He did so as if it had turned red hot. His expression was so tragic that her heart gave a little pang, which she fiercely suppressed. He would cause trouble with her fiancé now unless she took charge of the situation.

"Mr. Blake," she said brightly, "here is our friend Mr. Hightower, come to congratulate us."

"How considerate." Connor was not fooled; he recognized his predecessor and eyed him without warmth, taking Cecily by the elbow as if to show that she belonged to him.

Though Connor was no taller than Freddie, he had the advantage in age. Freddie's slender frame looked slight next to Connor's strong build. But she had to give him credit for courage: he looked his successor straight in the eye and offered his hand.

"I would wish you happiness, sir, but I know that with Miss Jaine at your side you will have all the happiness any man could ask for." Then he bowed to Cecily. "Your servant, ma'am."

The shop bell jingled as he exited to the street. For a moment Cecily was in danger of feeling forlorn. Perhaps sensing this, her fiancé cleared his throat.

"That must have been difficult, my dear."

She nodded, not trusting her voice.

Gently he tipped her chin up until she had to meet his gaze. His dark eyes were warm with understanding. "Would it cheer you up to see the magnificent set of pearls I've hired for you to wear at the wedding?"

"It might," she said, brightening.

"If you like them well enough, you might just be able to talk me into buying them outright."

"Then by all means, lead me to them," she said. She thought there was a special care and courtesy in the way he looked down at her, and she banished the last thought of her conversation with Freddie from her mind. Her future was safe in the hands of Connor Blake.

Events unfolded more quickly than she would have believed possible. She had noted before the lubricative powers of money, and evidently Mr. Blake was willing to spend what was necessary to prevent having to wait. Before she knew it she was standing in a registry office with him, signing her name while Cousin Margaret stood by, holding her bouquet and weeping happily into a lacy new handkerchief.

Connor had invited her to join them on her honeymoon, saying that Cecily might want company while he was conducting business. But Margaret was eager to retire to her little seaside cottage now that she had no need to worry about her charge.

That pleased Cecily perfectly well. So when she and her new husband boarded the train for their honeymoon, Cousin Margaret stood on the platform, waving them off.

She did not seem to be alone, though. Frowning, Cecily peered through the soot-smudged window of their compartment. Was that a flash of fair hair? She could not be certain, however, and by the time the train drew out of the station she had almost convinced herself she had been mistaken. For why would Freddie wish to see her off?

Linking her arm through her husband's, she set her mind to more pleasant subjects, like all the exciting destinations that lay ahead.

Once they were on the Continent, there was no lack of pleasant diversions to prevent her from dwelling on the past. Connor seemed to enjoy taking her shopping and encouraged her to buy anything that caught her fancy. He delighted in taking her along to business meetings and dinner appointments—showing her off, as she soon realized. Attired in one of her many lovely new dresses and gems to match, she could see the pride in his face when he presented her.

Later, when they were alone, he would exult over her success.

"They were all envious of me, to a man," he would tell her. "As how could they not be, with such a beautiful young creature for my wife?"

"You're exaggerating, I'm sure." But she enjoyed the compliment all the same.

"Not a whit. You've no idea what a picture you are—that creamy skin, those luminous eyes." He ran a fingertip along her bare shoulder, and smiled. "That willowy form."

Her triumphs fanned the flame of his ardency, and most nights ended in loving. As a lover he was both enthusiastic and tender, and with every passing hour the memory of Freddie Hightower grew fainter. Altogether Cecily found married life to be as close to heaven as earthly existence could permit.

That is, until they moved to Sterne House.

The conditions under which they took residence there, she had to admit, were far from ideal. After they returned to England there was an instance of error and confusion that required them to rush to take an earlier train than they had anticipated. After the sun-drenched Continent, the cold, wet English weather was especially dismal. The coach that met them at the station was old and leaky, so that rain-water seeped in as they were jounced over ruts in the road. By the time it rounded a curve in the road to reveal her new home, Cecily was wet, shivering, and miserable, and not at all in a receptive mood.

Especially when the house confronting her was so forbidding. On this bleak, rain-swept evening, the rough gray stone looked like cold made visible. The square towers with their crenelated tops would have better suited a fortress, not a home. Through some peculiarity in the lay of the land or the angle of the road, the massive place seemed to loom up over the carriage as it approached, as though at any moment it might come tumbling down and crush them.

Unnerved, she shrank back against Connor's side. "This is Sterne House?" she faltered.

"Yes," said her husband, and she recognized the note in his voice. It was pride. "Magnificent, isn't it?"

She shivered, and he drew her close to him.

"You will grow to love it, I know. In daylight you will see that it's more a castle than a house. And there is so much history here. Think of it—King Charles himself took refuge here during the days before his exile to France!"

"How thrilling," she said dutifully, but history seemed terribly remote. She wished for nothing but a hot bath by a roaring fire and then a soft bed warmed by a hot-water bottle—but unfortunately, as they soon discovered, none of these felicities had been prepared for them.

"We weren't expecting you 'til tomorrow," said the flustered little maid who opened the door to them.

"Didn't the housekeeper receive my letter?" Connor waved her away as she timidly approached to take his coat, and she turned her attention to Cecily.

"No, sir," she said as she helped Cecily out of her wet cloak. "We've not received any letter."

Connor's lips thinned. His anger could be cutting, and Cecily was glad she was not the one who displeased him. "Be so good as to ask Mrs. Ansley to come speak to me."

The maid bit her lip. "She isn't here, sir. She was called away on urgent business this morning. It was—"

"I shall get the full story from her in due time. Has a fire been laid in our rooms?"

"No, sir, as I said—"

"We weren't expected. Well, now that we are here, please see to it at once." He put his arm around Cecily, who sneezed, and his voice softened. "My wife mustn't take a chill."

"No, sir. Yes, sir. There is a fire laid in the drawing room, sir—I'll just set it alight." The young woman bobbed a curtsey and scampered off.

Heaving a sigh, Connor rubbed Cecily's arm. "I'm sorry, my dear. This isn't the welcome I had planned for you. Sterne House is not showing you its best face."

"I'll be all right," she said stoutly, but she was relieved when Connor led her to the drawing room, where the maid knelt by the hearth, coaxing the firewood alight.

The maid had lit a few candles in window sconces, but most of the room was dark. Cecily caught the glint of light on countless portraits that hung on the walls, their subjects naught but pale circles in the gloom. Elaborate plaster scrollwork decorated the mantel and cornice, and the busy shapes cast strange shadows as the fire leaped into life. She shivered.

"You must be frozen half to death," said Connor, observing this.

"It's mostly my feet," she said bravely. "If I could just get them warm, the rest wouldn't be so bad."

"Here, sit down by the fire and let's get your wet shoes and stockings off."

The maid had withdrawn. Cecily's fingers were so chilled they were stiff and clumsy, and she needed Connor's help in untying first her bootlaces and then her garters. Even though they had the room to themselves, she could feel herself blushing under the gaze of those ghostly ancestors on the walls as Connor's hands grazed her thighs.

But what he did next put self-consciousness out of her mind. Seating himself at her feet, he pulled his shirt front free of his trouser waistband. Then he took her ankles in his two hands and drew her feet beneath his shirt to rest on his chest.

The sudden warmth, but more especially the intimacy of it, kindled a different kind of heat in her veins. Against the soles of her feet she felt the tickle of his chest hair and the rise and fall of his breathing. Watching her face, he ran his hands up and down her shins, stroking the cold away.

"Better?"

She nodded. "But you'll be even colder now."

In the firelight his eyes were hooded, but his mouth moved in a smile. "It doesn't matter."

All her life she had tried to please other people and put their comfort before hers. She had subjugated her own needs and desires even to the point of never so much as asking for a sip of water unless it was offered her. And now here was this man, treating her as though she was treasured. It brought a lump to her throat.

"What's wrong?" he asked.

"Nothing. I was just thinking how fortunate I am to have such a husband. That's all."

His hands stilled on her legs. His eyes were still in shadow, but she heard him murmur an endearment as, putting her legs to one side, he rose to his knees and gathered her to him.

She had no further difficulty with being cold that night.

Waking early the next morning and finding herself unable to go back to sleep, Cecily went exploring in her dressing gown.

The bedroom she and Connor shared was hung in dark blue damask, and there were more of those unsettling family portraits on the walls. Averting her gaze, Cecily slipped into the hallway and carefully shut the door behind her, doing her best to prevent it from creaking. Connor was still sleeping.

She was curious to learn whether her new home was as hostile by day as it had been by night. It was certainly dim, for no daylight penetrated into the corridor outside her bedroom. The gas jets had been lit, however, and she went to adjust one to bring up the light. As the illumination brightened, Cecily's eyes grew round at the grandeur of her new home.

Thick carpets in jewel colors cushioned her footsteps, and the walls were hung with antique tapestries. Between the tapestries, huge mirrors in heavy gilded frames reflected her image back to her: she looked small and pale in the midst of so much splendor. Almost like a ghost. Could the house have ghosts? As old as it was, she would not be surprised if tragic and mysterious events had taken place there. She would have to ask Connor.

"Madam?"

Cecily started. The thick carpet had muffled the approaching footsteps of a tall, black-clad woman with a chatelaine of keys—the housekeeper, evidently. "You startled me!" she exclaimed.

"I apologize, madam. I am the housekeeper, Mrs. Ansley. I hope you were not put to any great inconvenience by my absence upon your arrival."

Her manner was courteous but not warm. Her gray eyes were busy sizing up her mistress but did not reveal anything about her conclusions. Cecily, for her part, was doing some sizing up herself. The housekeeper might have been anywhere from thirty to fifty, although this might have been the aging effect of her unfashionable dress, whose skirt was supported by petticoats instead of a fashionable crinoline. Her dark hair was tidy beneath its white cap, and Cecily was all the more aware of her own tumbled hair and dressing gown. What a slovenly creature she must look to the housekeeper.

"I am so glad to make your acquaintance, Mrs. Ansley," she said. "I know I have a great deal to learn about the running of a household, and I will rely on you to teach me. I hope that we shall become the best of friends."

She was being too eager, too gushing, but she couldn't seem to stop. The housekeeper must have been put off by her effort to ingratiate herself, for her reply was cool: "I shall do my best, of course, madam."

Cecily squirmed inwardly. This was starting out on the wrong foot. But before she could try to correct her course, even if she had known how, the housekeeper spoke again. "I came to tell you that breakfast will be laid for you and the master in the small family dining room in a quarter of an hour."

"Thank you. Er—could you possibly send a maid to show me the way? I haven't had a chance to learn my way around yet."

"Of course, madam. And after you and the master have eaten I shall be happy to give you a tour."

"Oh, that would be lovely. I imagine it will take me ages to learn where everything is. The first Mrs. Blake must have had the same difficulty!" She was babbling again. What was it about that remote, courteous gaze that made her exert herself so foolishly?

The housekeeper did not laugh at her small joke. Instead she said, "Sterne House belonged to the family of the first Mrs. Blake, going back more than two centuries. My late mistress was familiar with the property from the time she was a girl."

So much for any common ground Cecily might have felt with her predecessor. If the late Mrs. Blake had grown up in these surroundings, she must have been a rather grand creature. How would she have felt, knowing that she had been succeeded by someone so insignificant? She might have looked at Cecily much as Mrs. Ansley was doing now— as if she were too childish and unsophisticated for her new position as the wife of Connor Blake.

But perhaps she was letting her own nervousness rule her imagination. She might as well find out. "What was the first Mrs. Blake like?" she asked.

The housekeeper's gaze flickered and turned inward. Somehow she had become even more remote than before. "She was a gracious and worthy lady," she said, "but it is painful to think about her. I think you'll find that the late Mrs. Blake is a topic that none of the staff will wish to discuss."

Well, there was a snub if Cecily had ever heard one. Apparently her very natural curiosity about her predecessor was destined to go unsatisfied.

Having struck her silent, the housekeeper excused herself and withdrew. Cecily bit her thumbnail and wondered if she would ever manage to thaw the woman or if this first unfortunate meeting would set the tone for their entire relationship.

If only Cecily had had some training for her new position. She would have felt less out of place and would have seemed better suited in the eyes of Mrs. Ansley.

Still gnawing her thumbnail, she looked at the wall of portraits that confronted her. The first Mrs. Blake's distinguished ancestors, most likely. Though less eerie by daylight, their pale, stiff faces nonetheless seemed to sneer down at her as unworthy to live in their ancestral home.

As she looked, there was a strange sound and a faint movement. She jumped back just in time to avoid being struck by one of the portraits as it fell. The heavy frame struck the floor with a force she could feel through the soles of her feet.

She had given an involuntary yelp, and now she stared wide-eyed at the fallen portrait. The heavy frame could have bruised or even crushed her toes.

"Madam? Are you all right?" The breathless words belonged to a young woman in a maid's uniform, who rushed up to her in alarm.

"Quite all right, er..."

"Janet, madam." The girl curtseyed.

"Quite all right, Janet." She gave a laugh, albeit a shaky one, as she regarded the fallen painting. "I suppose this sort of thing happens often in a house as old as this one."

"Oh no, madam." The girl's wide blue eyes rebuked her. "Everything is kept shipshape and proper as you please. I've never seen this happen before." Moving to the wall, she touched the paper where the painting had hung. "It looks as though the nail came loose. I can have one of the men see to it, madam."

"Thank you, Janet." But she couldn't resist the opportunity to test Mrs. Ansley's words. "Would you say the late Mrs. Blake resembled these portraits?"

Janet's gaze flicked to her and then quickly away. "Why... that is... I really couldn't say, madam."

She was so clearly uncomfortable that Cecily took pity on her. "For her sake, I hope she did not resemble any of these characters," she said. "Not a very comely lot, are they?"

Janet's expression cleared, and she giggled. "I should say not, madam! Especially that old fellow in the powdered wig. He looks more like a fish than a man."

Before Cecily could reply, Connor's voice came unexpectedly. "It's time you returned to your duties, Janet," he said, and Cecily found that, unbeknownst to her, he had joined them. He was fully dressed for riding and looked powerful and commanding in his polished black boots. "Run along now," he told the maid, and Cecily wondered why he sounded so cold.

Janet curtseyed hastily and scurried from the room. "Talkative little creature," Connor said as she vanished through a door in the corner. "I hope she didn't bore you too much."

"No, she seems a sweet girl." Sweet, but nervous. Contrary to the housekeeper's warning, the maid hadn't looked sad when Cecily raised the subject of the first Mrs. Blake. She had looked ill at ease.

What on earth could be the cause of that? There had been the startling accident of the painting falling, but in itself that was insufficient cause for nerves.

Her husband's voice broke into her thoughts. "I would prefer it if you weren't quite so friendly with the servants," he said, leading her back down the hall to their bedroom.

"Why not?"

"Well, it isn't really their place to treat their mistress with such familiarity. It's very close to disrespect."

Cecily thought about the houses she had visited in which the servants and the mistress were at odds with each other. They had been highly uncomfortable places. The last thing she wanted was for her own home to have that hostile atmosphere. "I think I would rather risk a little bit of disrespect than be regarded without any affection," she said.

He smiled down at her. "Isn't it enough that you have my affection?"

She began to say that it wasn't the same thing. But it would be wise to let him have the last word, she suspected. As a wife, she must accustom herself to doing so.

"You are entirely right," she said. "Tell me, what shall we do today?"

He tucked her hand through his arm, looking well pleased with her answer. "After you've dressed and we've had breakfast, let's take a turn about the grounds," he said. "I want to show you all the improvements still to come."

"Goodness, how many will there be?"

"As many as necessary." There was determination in his eyes. "I intend for Sterne House to be a showplace that will be talked about through the length and breadth of England. And you, my dear, are to be the jewel in this setting." As he led her toward the bedchamber door, he said, "I want the name of Connor Blake to be spoken with admiration and envy, because of his wife as well as his estate."

It was a bit of a tall order. Nevertheless, the fact that he believed she could shoulder such a role made her determined to help his wish come true.

CHAPTER FOUR
Eleanor

Strangely enough, it was Connor Blake who brought the shocking news of her father's death.

It was late afternoon, and Eleanor was reading the latest issue of the *Lancet* in the drawing room, making notes in the margins with a pencil. She had no expectation of visitors and was wearing one of her oldest frocks, and when a commotion came to her ears she looked up, frowning.

Alice, the parlormaid, was saying, "Sir, if you'll wait until I ask the mistress—" and then the door burst open. Eleanor found herself on her feet, one hand going to her untidy hair, at the sight of Connor Blake. He put the maid aside, not ungently, and crossed the intervening space in two strides, it seemed, to take Eleanor's hand. The *Lancet* dropped to the floor.

He had clearly come directly from the building site. In shirtsleeves, he bore the dust of construction on his face and his boots, so that even before she fully took in his expression she knew that something urgent must have happened.

"You may leave us, Alice," she said, and was only dimly aware of the door closing behind the girl. Connor took her other hand in his. His dark eyes were full of a strange shocked sorrow, and his chest rose and fell as though he had run all the way there. But all of her confused impressions all fell away when he spoke the worst words he could have spoken.

"It's your father," he said.

Her heart gave a great thud in her breast. "An accident?"

"No one quite knows how it happened. A block of granite fell from atop the scaffolding, striking him on the head."

"I must go to him." Where was her bag? If she left now, she could probably be with him before a doctor. She made to ring the bell, but he would not release her hands, and in confusion she sought the reason in his eyes.

They regarded her unflinchingly. "Miss Fairley. There is nothing to be done."

"You cannot know that. If I can see to him right away, perhaps—"

"No." The starkness of the refusal made her stare, but his voice was as gentle as ever. "Please believe me when I say that your father is beyond help. Not even the most skilled surgeon on earth could recover him now. I don't wish to distress you, but you must understand that he is gone."

Her knees gave out, and she collapsed to the carpet in a whoosh of skirts. Without releasing her hands, he knelt before her.

"Gone," she repeated.

"I'm afraid so. I'm sorry, Miss Fairley."

The room was so quiet that she could hear her own blood sing in her ears. Dazed, she found herself staring at a patch of soot on the wainscoting. She must have one of the maids scrub that away. That so minor a thing could be remedied but her father's life could not be reclaimed made no sense.

"I must see him," she said. It would not be real to her until she saw him.

Connor flinched. He tried to hide it, but she saw it nonetheless, and it made her heart sink. "Frankly, I would not advise it," he said. "Not until he has been made fit for viewing. It is a horrifying sight. I shall never forget it myself."

If a soldier, a veteran of the wars, had found it so shocking, it must have been dreadful. She tried not to envision it, but her head was crowded with gruesome images from medical texts. "How could this happen?" she burst out. "All he did was go to look at a building. It isn't as though he went into a mine, or a battle."

"I am so sorry. It oughtn't to have happened." All at once his arms were around her as they knelt there on the rug, and she found unexpected comfort in the strength of his embrace. With her cheek pressed against his chest she felt the reassurance of his breathing. "Do you have someone to stay with you?" he asked, in a lower tone. "A friend or relation I could send for?"

She shook her head, and the linen of his shirt brushed her cheek. "I've no one," she said dully. Her father was—had been—her truest friend.

That made him draw back, and perhaps unconsciously his hand went to her cheek as his eyes searched hers. "You mustn't be left alone," he whispered. "No one should be made to bear so great a loss in solitude."

"Stay with me, then." The words were out before they had even formed in her mind, but once spoken they seemed the most logical thing in the world.

"I would do so and gladly, Eleanor. But there is your reputation to consider. I'll not wreck your social standing on top of everything else." He touched his lips to her forehead in the gentlest of caresses. "I had best be off. Alice will see to you." But when he made to rise and draw her to her feet, she clung to his hand.

"You and Papa were close," she said. "He was so attached to you. You more than anyone know how kind and—and how wonderful he was. You must stay. Even if it is just for a few hours. You're the only one who can understand." She realized that tears were sliding down her cheeks, and when after only slight hesitation he drew her toward him again, she clung to him, finding a wisp of solace in the broad solidity of his chest. When everything she knew seemed to be falling away, the warm strength of his embrace was a place of safety.

His voice came softly. "Then I shall stay," he said, and held her close until, an unknowable time later, a doctor came to confirm the news that Connor had already broken.

It was old Dr. Carmody, whom Eleanor had known all her life, and the grim look in his eyes convinced her that there was no mistake, no room for uncertainty, and her father was really lost to her.

"I see the news has reached you," he said, and her eyes blurred with a sudden new rush of tears.

"Did he suffer?" she managed to ask.

"No, my dear child. Death was instantaneous."

"I would like to see him."

Like Connor, however, the doctor was discouraging. "Wait until he has been tidied up. The damage to his skull was devastating," he said, and though his candor made her wince, she was grateful for it. At least she could stop fearing that her father's injury would not have been fatal if he had received prompt medical attention. Dr. Carmody glanced at Connor, still a steadying presence by her side. "I'm glad you've someone to stay with you, my dear. The coming days and weeks will be less difficult for you."

"Oh, but—"

"Perhaps your fiancé will be good enough to inform the staff of your father's passing and take that unhappy duty off your shoulders."

Connor assented, and the doctor tipped his hat, offered a last crisp phrase of condolence, and departed too quickly for her to correct his misapprehension. No doubt he dreaded tears and hysterics. It was all too clear why he had made such a mistake; who but her future husband would have his arm about her waist? Belatedly she realized how improper this was, and she moved slightly away from him.

"You needn't be the one to inform the staff," he said, misunderstanding her movement. "The doctor's idea was sound, even if he did not quite understand the nature of our friendship."

I'm not certain I understand it myself, she thought. "No, I must be the one to tell them," she said. "But I should take it as a kindness if you would stay with me while I do so."

"Of course I shall, Eleanor."

It was not the first time, she realized, that he had called her by her Christian name. She ought to have found it presumptuous, but instead it was comforting in its intimacy.

They descended into the servants' quarters, and the startled housekeeper sent Alice to gather the rest of the servants at Eleanor's request. In short order all were assembled in the staff dining room, crowding in to stand around the long dining table.

In a few short sentences Eleanor explained what had happened. The words sounded strange to her, as though someone else were saying them. At first the servants stood in shocked silence.

Then Lamb, the butler, said gravely, "We are heartily sorry to hear it, miss. Mr. Fairley was a good man and a kind and just employer, God rest his soul."

There was an echoing murmur among the others. Then Alice ventured, "What's to happen to us, miss?"

For a second Eleanor could only stare at her. It had not occurred to her until now, so paralyzed had her brain been, that she held the fate of all of these people in her hands.

"I can't think very far into the future just now," she said, "but I cannot imagine I'll be leaving this house. All of you who wish to stay will continue to have a place here. If I should ever decide to settle elsewhere, naturally I shall make certain to find you new places first. I know that—that my father would have done the same."

Her voice broke, and Connor stepped forward, putting a hand to her back to steady her. "Your mistress would be the better for a hot posset," he told the cook, who wiped her eyes with a corner of her apron and bustled away.

Eleanor let Connor lead her back upstairs and to the sitting room. Dusk was setting in, but Alice had not yet drawn the drapes, distracted no doubt by the events of the day, so Connor went around the room and drew them closed with an air of protecting the privacy of Eleanor's grief. She took a seat on the divan near the fireplace, where a paper fan guarded a tidy arrangement of logs.

"Do you wish for the fire to be lit?"

She did not answer. At this time of day she and her father were usually reading companionably here, he chuckling over *Household Words*, she absorbed in a medical journal. Even though half an hour might pass without their exchanging a word, it was the coziest part of her day. And from now on she would have to pass it alone.

A low groan broke from her, and she hid her face in her hands. It was unbearable.

A light touch on one of her hands made her look up. Connor stood before her, his face grave.

"Forgive me," he said, "but I must leave you. Would you like me to ring for someone to sit with you?"

Dismay and realization flooded through her. Of course he could not stay with her indefinitely; he had other responsibilities and probably social engagements as well. Perhaps even an appointment with a sweetheart.

"I've been selfish," she said. "I never thought to ask if you had obligations elsewhere. You have been more than generous already, and I cannot thank you enough for helping me endure these first hours." Nevertheless the prospect of his leaving wrenched her heart.

"You mistake me," he said gently. "I meant only to leave you long enough to make myself tidy and remedy the shortcomings in my attire." With a wry half smile and a gesture he indicated his rough clothing. "I can return within the hour if you wish it."

She had long since stopped noticing that he was still dusty and clad in shirtsleeves, but he must have been uncomfortably aware of the impropriety of such a costume, and her conscience reproached her.

Still, it might be only a pretext. He was too tactful to flaunt a rendezvous in the face of her mourning. Or—more likely—he was thinking again of her reputation if he should extend his call past nightfall. It was a kind thought, an honorable thought. Yet the prospect of spending the rest of the evening alone made her want to clutch at him with both hands.

He must have seen her inner struggle reflected in her face, for he said, "If you prefer, I could direct one of your servants to my quarters to fetch more suitable clothing."

"Yes," she exclaimed, so quickly that it embarrassed her. "That is—unless you are concerned about the neighbors talking. I suppose it won't do either of our reputations any good for you to stay."

For some reason, that made him smile down at her. His dark eyes gazing into hers, he said, "But there is no cause for tongues to wag when a lady's betrothed husband lingers at her home."

Perhaps her brain was too numb from the emotional battering of the day, for she could not seem to comprehend his meaning. "Betrothed?"

He seated himself beside her and took her hands in his. "Your Dr. Carmody had the right idea," he said softly. "I want nothing more than to look after you and protect you, not just tonight but every night. I want to help shoulder your sorrow so that it weighs less heavily on you. And I want, some day, to make you happy again."

Bending his head, he put his lips to hers with such gentleness that it was more promise than kiss. She could not breathe. Her heartbeat drummed in her ears, and when she opened her eyes to him a strange, piercing sweetness rushed into her heart.

It was the worst time to make so vital a decision, she knew. Now, when her mind and her heart were exhausted from shock and sorrow. She ought to take a few days, at least, to think it over.

Then she thought of her promise to her father. It seemed strangely prophetic now, almost as if he had known that soon she would need the strength and comfort a husband could offer. And not just any husband. This man. Connor Blake, who was sitting beside her now, his eyes gazing into hers with urgent intensity.

"Yes?" he whispered.

Caution gave one last warning flicker and died.

"Yes," she said.

The funeral baked meats did coldly furnish forth the marriage table. She could not help but think of the line from *Hamlet* when she and Connor married the day after her father's funeral. There were few well-wishers at their wedding breakfast; Mr. March, her father's secretary, was at hand, having worked closely with Connor on the details of the funeral and plans for the wedding tour. Eleanor had been contented to leave all of that in their hands. No, *contented* was the wrong word; it was more as if she were in a daze, and her mind could not quite grasp concrete details like schedules, invitations, and appointments.

Once embarked on their wedding tour, they always seemed to be encountering distinguished people that her father had known or that Connor recognized, and almost every night they were having dinner with their new acquaintances. Eleanor realized that her husband must have planned these encounters to offer stimulation for her, to take her mind off her grief, and she smiled as she listened to his conversation, as he had even taken pains to learn something of their new friends. There were Benton Carbey, the distinguished barrister, and Mrs. Caleb Fitzsimmons, the social arbiter of London, who took Eleanor aside to tell her in approving tones what a handsome and charming husband she had.

As for when she and her husband were alone, that was pleasure of another sort.

From her medical studies, she was aware of the physical reality of conjugal life. She had not been prepared, however, for the sensations awakened when her husband embraced her, the languorous heat that spread through her limbs, the tingling of her skin. And while she had expected to find the act embarrassing when it came to pass, the beauty of his body—both to the eye and to the touch—distracted her from such self-consciousness. She had surprised both of them with her eagerness, and he had greeted it as a boon, not as some mark of unwomanliness. Yes, she was quite happy with married life.

It saddened her, though, that her new happiness was commingled with grief for her father. How he would have loved this tour! He would have taken such pleasure in exploring and seeking out the architectural highlights of each town and city. Eleanor asked Connor once if he would not like to spend more time in Florence visiting the fine Palladian homes, knowing her father would have wished to do so, but he had not seemed interested.

By that point she was becoming homesick, and Connor duly made arrangements for their return.

So it was that one evening in September she found herself in a carriage jolting over a rutted, ill-kept road, only to finally arrive at...Sterne House?

Disbelieving, she stared at the blank, hostile facade and its narrow, suspicious windows. The square towers made her think of sieges and battles, and the rough surface of the stone put her in mind of diseased skin pitted with sores.

"Why are we here?" she exclaimed.

Her husband had been examining some papers by the dim light admitted by the carriage window. "I thought the house in Surrey would be too depressing for you," he said, raising his head. "I'm sure it holds countless memories of your life with your father."

Which was why she would have found it comforting—the very opposite of her associations with Sterne House.

But she did not want to reject his kindness. "I shall probably become accustomed in time," she said. "Perhaps a short stay at Sterne will prepare me to return to Surrey."

He patted her hand. "There's no need to force yourself, my dear. You may find that starting fresh here suits you admirably, especially once we spruce up the place so that we may welcome guests."

"I'm still in mourning," she said, startled by this vision of their future. "I don't think anyone would expect us to entertain."

He waved a hand dismissively. "I mean once you are ready, of course."

She had never had a love of entertaining; simply having one or two friends to dinner was as grand as she and her father had ever cared to be. She tried to envision this ugly, hostile house as a destination for guests and the location of house parties, and she could not.

Indoors it was no better than she had remembered. Cold drafts whistled through cracks in the walls, and the crumbling flagstones of the entrance hall threatened to trip her. The upper reaches of the vast hall were in shadow, but she fancied she saw the movement of something that might have been bats.

Drawing her cloak tight about her, she asked, "Did you have the staff from the Surrey house brought in?"

"March made all the arrangements. I'm not certain how many of them wished to come all the way out here."

So she might even be denied the comfort of familiar faces. It gave her a pang, but she could understand why they might wish to stay behind. "And the new staff?"

"Locals, or so I believe. I'm certain March got the best people available." Seeing doubt in her face, he squeezed her hand. "If any of them turns out to be unfit, we can look for someone new. But do give them a chance, my dear. I imagine they will be more than adequate for our modest needs."

She tried to keep an open mind as the evening wore on, but she recognized none of the servants who attended her. Moreover, her new surroundings were no cheerier than she remembered from her childhood visits. Floorboards creaked and popped in rooms where fires were being lit for the first time in years, making her jump and look around for intruders. Window draperies stirred in the draft like the sails of foundered ships slowly being claimed by a ravenous ocean. Some of the wooden ceiling beams, she knew, had been torn from wounded ships, and doubtless other features of the house as well. Even now she could not quite escape her childhood fancy that in the night the drowned sailors would enter the house to reclaim this booty.

Happily, however, there was an antidote to her fears that she had not had as a child: sympathetic companionship. When she climbed into the chilly tester bed next to her husband and he slipped his arms around her, the phantoms receded and her mood brightened.

She could tolerate the inconvenience and gloom for a short while, she decided. What did the house's shortcomings matter in what, after all, was only to be a brief visit?

"Connor," she whispered.

"Yes?"

"Thank you for arranging everything. It was very thoughtful of you."

"I just want you to be happy, my dear. And there is one more thing."

"What's that?"

He stroked her hair back from her forehead, and in the moonlight spilling through a crack in the drapes she could see him smiling at her. "If the three-fingered lady should venture into our chambers," he said, "I'm quite prepared to fight her off with the fireplace poker."

She laughed and kissed him, and the evening was not ruined after all.

CHAPTER FIVE
Cecily

It was heavenly to Cecily to have her own home, to never have to wonder where her next meal was coming from, to know that she would always be warm and comfortable and cared for. She took pride in the grandeur of the house and was fascinated by the planned improvements and additions that Connor was embarked upon.

But there were disadvantages. Having expected—not unreasonably, she thought—to be mistress of the house, she was taken aback to find that Connor made all decisions, right down to which set of china should be used when they entertained. When she had resolved to help him make Sterne House enviable, she had imagined she would actually be able to participate in that endeavor.

Perhaps because he considered the property his public face, he was devoted to making improvements to it—bringing it up to date with extensive gas lighting, adding a new wing, creating the artificial lake, and the like. It seemed that the sound of hammering and sawing and workers' voices shouting to each other was present whenever she stirred outside the house, and she knew that soon they would be inside as well. But if she spoke to Connor of having a headache from the noise or wondered if they could not do without some of his planned improvements, he would look at her rebukingly and say, "Sterne House needs a mistress who wishes to put its best face forward" or, even worse, "I expected better of you, Cecily." When he said such things she could not help but suspect that he was comparing her to her predecessor and finding her wanting.

His former marriage was certainly another unwelcome element in her life, for Connor's first wife seemed to never leave Cecily's mind. She was conspicuous in her absence when Connor and the servants so obviously avoided speaking of her. Nor was her taste evident in the decorations or furnishings, for whenever Cecily asked about the provenance of some object she learned it had been with the house since time immemorial, or that her husband had chosen it. Through careful questioning Cecily learned that the rooms formerly occupied by Connor and his first wife had been shut up, and that the bedchamber and dressing rooms he and Cecily now inhabited had been furnished and decorated just for her.

With all traces of her predecessor thus erased, Cecily was uncertain why she felt her presence so keenly. Perhaps the main form this took was a sensation of being watched.

It began very early in their tenancy at Sterne House. The first time, as best she could recall, was when she was in the morning room, which was supposed to be her own domain. Opening a drawer of the cherrywood desk, she reached in for writing paper and drew out a letter.

It was unsigned and unfinished, but the hand was feminine and learned, and as soon as she saw the contents she realized who the writer had to be.

My dear Dr. Grant, it began,
I must be brief. To my dismay, my husband shows no inclination to change his mind or even to

permit me to speak with you again. Indeed, he has
been most vehement, and I fear

The letter broke off there with a splatter of ink, and Cecily regarded it with curiosity. There was a whiff of conspiracy about it that fascinated her. Had Connor's first wife been out to chisel money from him? Perhaps with the aid of a lover? She wondered who this doctor was, and whether he lived in the vicinity. If she could find him, perhaps she would learn what kind of a woman her predecessor had been.

With her thoughts thus busy, she heard a soft noise and looked up, expecting to find Mrs. Ansley hovering in the doorway, hoping to catch her attention. But no one was there.

No one that she could see, at least. But the nature of the room's silence had changed. The hairs at the back of her neck rose, and she felt certain that she was being watched.

She took a slow, thorough look about the room, noting that there were no hiding places, no armoires or high-backed settees or anything of the like. The drapes were drawn back, and no one could have been concealed behind them.

No doubt it was just fancy. A mouse in the wainscoting, aided by her silly imagination and the dead-eyed portraits that adorned the walls. Her husband seemed to have a positive fascination with them, but she had not yet learned to like them.

With a shrug she replaced the letter in the desk drawer, thinking to show it to the housekeeper to see if she would at least confirm the handwriting as that of her former mistress. But she forgot to mention it the next time she saw Mrs. Ansley, and it was soon driven out of her mind by stranger incidents, like the unnerving episode that took place after she persuaded the housekeeper to take her on a tour of the house.

The room she was most interested in was the one that had belonged to the first Mrs. Blake, but in order to disguise that interest she pretended to wish to see the entire house, from garret to granary. Cecily made the appropriate admiring comments on the newly refurbished entrance hall, formal dining room, tapestried gallery, and other features sure to awe visitors, and tried not to show her distaste for the drafty, dismal, broken-down rooms that had been shut up instead of being restored. It struck her as peculiar that the house had two such distinct personalities, as it were, but she was all the more impressed by the work her husband had done to make a showplace of Sterne House.

Even though they omitted the areas that were unsafe, it was a very long tour. When the housekeeper at last stopped at the door to the bedchamber of Cecily's predecessor and said, "This was the first Mrs. Blake's room," the afternoon was drawing in.

"I should love to see the inside," Cecily said, and sensed tension in the housekeeper.

"I'm afraid Mr. Blake has forbidden me to open the room, madam. I cannot go against his orders."

She offered her most charming smile. "Not even for me?"

The housekeeper, alas, did not seem susceptible to charm. "I'm afraid not, madam. Indeed, I no longer have the key."

Now, was she telling the truth, or had she resorted to a lie so that she would not be torn between the opposing wills of master and mistress? Under Cecily's thoughtful gaze she dropped her eyes. "If you'll excuse me, madam, I must go make certain Effie has ironed the table linens," she murmured.

"Very well." Cecily made no move to leave, and the housekeeper made a stiff courtesy and withdrew down the corridor.

When she was out of sight and the jingle of her keys had faded from her hearing, Cecily tried the handle of the door, twisting it most vigorously, and even tried shaking it. To no avail; the door was set firmly in its frame, and it would not yield.

The room next door, though. Might that offer a way in? If it had been a nursery or dressing room, it might adjoin the first Mrs. Blake's bedroom, and perhaps the housekeeper had not thought about locking it.

To her surprise, the next door over was in fact unlocked. Then, when she pushed it open, she saw scaffolding and boards and tarpaulins and realized that the room was undergoing renovation. No workmen were there at present, though, so she did not feel the need to rush as she looked around.

And her diligence was rewarded: half concealed behind the scaffolding was another door. It was painted and papered to blend in with the surrounding wall, but the outlines were clear. There was no handle, so she found a pair of pliers among the workers' tools and used them to get a sufficient grip on the lock plate to draw it open. The hinges were stiff and it would not open far, but Cecily was able to slip through it.

This room, evidently the bedroom, was darker, as the drapes were nearly closed. Her first thought as her eyes adjusted was that it was a very plain room. She soon realized that this was because it seemed to have been looted. There were few pictures on the walls, leading Cecily to speculate that they had been removed for use in other rooms. Yet other items remained untouched, like the silver and tortoiseshell vanity set, which though dark with tarnish lay all anyhow on the dressing table as though they had just been set down by their mistress. Cecily picked up the hairbrush, which had been lying with its bristles down, and replaced it with the bristles turned up, though it was unlikely it would ever be used again and thus preserving the bristles served no purpose. It simply irritated her to see the brush placed incorrectly.

She opened the armoire and found a few other items left behind: a wrinkled length of ribbon, a single lace cuff. Probably the clothes had been given away or put into storage. It was a pity, because Cecily would have loved to see what knowledge of the woman's character could be gleaned from her clothing. She wondered if there was anyone who could tell her what had been done with the clothes.

Across the room, as she continued to explore, she found a few last items that might give her an idea of the room's former inhabitant. On the wall was a small framed photograph of a genial-looking older man with a white beard. A relation, perhaps? There was also a photograph of Connor, the same one that Cecily had on her own dressing table. Something was different about this one, though. Frowning, she leaned forward and prodded at the frame with one finger. Almost invisible, tucked at the edge of the frame was what appeared to be a curved sewing needle. What a curious thing to find there. A memento of some kind? If so, what could it mean?

Her train of thought was interrupted when a draft touched the lace at her throat, making her shiver. From somewhere behind her came a tiny, distinct tap.

Startled, she turned to find the room seemingly unchanged. The door still stood partly ajar, but no one else had entered. What had caused the sound?

In any case, it was time she left. She would not like to have to explain to her husband why she was lurking around this room when he had proven so reluctant to even mention his first wife. She crossed to the door, glancing around to see if there was anything she had missed.

Then she saw the brush. Somehow, while her back was turned, it had been turned over and placed back in its original position, bristles down. The tap she had heard must have been the silver handle coming to rest on the dusty wooden surface.

A shiver tightened her scalp.

"Hello?" she said tentatively. "Is someone there?"

There was no sound, but for no reason she could have explained she felt that she was not alone.

It couldn't be a ghost, she told herself. Nonetheless, without pausing to look any further, she darted toward the door. Slipping through it, she shut it swiftly so that anything in the room could not follow her.

The renovations continued, to her irritation. But it began to seem as though the workers were irritating more than just her. Every day men came to Connor complaining of tools disappearing, of mysterious accidents that kept delaying their work. Cecily, sipping tea while the foreman complained to her husband during breakfast one day, was privately amused.

"It sounds as if the house is protecting itself," she said after the foreman had gone stomping off, dissatisfied.

Connor glanced at her as he helped himself to more toast. "What is that supposed to mean?"

"Oh, merely that the house may not wish to be modernized. You know how intractable and set in their ways these old piles become." She laughed, but he did not join in.

"That sounds like superstition," he said. "Next you'll be saying that a ghost is at work."

She knew he meant it jokingly, but the idea struck her with unease. Might the ghost of some Cavalier be resisting having his family home invaded by workmen? Or perhaps it was more personal. Perhaps the spirit of the first Mrs. Blake did not want her widower improving the house for her successor. Though Cecily was far from certain that she believed in ghosts, she knew she had not imagined what she had seen and heard in Eleanor Blake's bedchamber.

She was determined to satisfy her curiosity at least in part. So she chose an evening when Connor was in away on business and cornered the housekeeper well after the evening meal, when she suspected the servants would have finished eating and the housekeeper would have retired to her private sitting room.

Mrs. Ansley's blank, almost panicked look when she opened her sitting-room door to find Cecily there told her that she knew something. Cecily smiled ingratiatingly and held up a length of fine wool melton.

"Good evening, Mrs. Ansley. I wanted to discuss something with you concerning the maid's uniforms. May I come in?"

Naturally the woman had no choice but to invite her mistress inside. It was a cozy little room, heated by a pot-bellied iron stove, and warmed by red curtains and a red-and-gold braided rug. "Please have a seat, Mrs. Blake," said Mrs. Ansley, indicating a chair. Only after her mistress had been seated did the housekeeper resume her seat in a rocking chair. On the small adjacent table were a lamp and a book. Cecily had rather expected needlework, not reading, but chastised herself for making assumptions.

Cecily's pretext for visiting was to discuss fabric for new uniforms for the servants, but as she talked she could tell that the housekeeper's mind was as little focused on the topic as her own. After a maid brought in tea, Cecily took the opportunity while the housekeeper was pouring it out to venture upon the topic that really interested her.

"I know it is a sad subject, but I would like to learn more about my predecessor," she said. "What sort of person she was, how I can best honor her memory. I hate to bother you with it, but my husband refuses to speak of her at all. You know how men can be."

As soon as the words were spoken she realized that Mrs. Ansley might never have been married, and her title might be merely the conventional appellation for her position.

But the housekeeper did not correct her. It seemed to Cecily that Mrs. Ansley was taking a very long time to pour out the tea and add sugar, perhaps to avoid meeting Cecily's eyes. But at last the woman handed Cecily her tea, sat back in her chair with an almost inaudible sigh, and looked straight at her employer.

Interestingly, what Cecily saw was not grief. It was wariness. What was she afraid to divulge?

"I shall tell you what I can," she said, and again Cecily sensed a guarded air. "But I must remind you that I only knew the first Mrs. Blake for a short time, and only in my capacity as servant. My relationship with her was not an intimate one."

"That is fine," Cecily said, trying to curb her eagerness. "Anything you can tell me is better than nothing. Was she very grand?"

The housekeeper blinked as if ambushed by something unexpected. "Well... er, no, I would not say so. She was dignified, and attractive, but with no airs at all. She liked to be useful."

That surprised Cecily. "Would you say she was a kind person?"

"Oh, very much so. And highly intelligent. She read very widely."

"So she and Mr. Blake must have enjoyed entertaining important people and hosting intellectual discussions." That was certainly what he seemed to wish for Cecily.

But the housekeeper shook her head. She seemed to be more confident than before; evidently this was not what she had feared discussing. "Mrs. Blake—Mrs. Eleanor, I should say—was in mourning for her father and did not feel equal to much entertaining."

"She wished for a quiet life? Seclusion?"

"I would not say that, exactly. She seemed to miss her life in Surrey and the friends and patients she left behind. She was a trained nurse."

"A nurse!" That stymied her. Why a woman who could afford to live a leisured existence would wish to involve herself in a world of pain, disease, and horror made no sense to her at all. But perhaps Eleanor Blake had actually been that altruistic...and eccentric.

More to the point, she did not sound like someone whose spirit would linger after death to torment those who lived in her house.

"Mrs. Eleanor was an unusual lady," the housekeeper said, evidently observing her confusion.

Cecily mulled this over. "You miss her," she observed.

Before the other woman could respond, there was a rapid knocking at the door. "Mrs. Ansley?" one of the maids called. "Cook needs you right away!"

"One moment." Mrs. Ansley rose, and Cecily did as well. "Please excuse me, madam."

"Of course." Cecily watched as the housekeeper went to the door and, after conferring briefly with the maid, went rapidly down the passage. The maid was about to do the same when Cecily recognized her. It was Janet. Here was a prime opportunity to glean more about Connor's first wife.

"Janet, can you help me a moment?" she said quickly. "I think a seam in my dress is coming loose. Perhaps you can repair it before it gets worse."

"Right away, madam," said Janet. "I'll just fetch the sewing basket—"

"I'm sure Mrs. Ansley has one here. Please come in and close the door."

The girl did so, though with a puzzled air. "Where is the loose seam, madam?" she asked, her eyes darting over Cecily's dress.

Cecily patted the seat of the rocking chair. "I just remembered it's in a different dress. But as long as you're here, I should love to learn more about the late Mrs. Blake."

Janet gave her an apprehensive look. She had not seated herself. "Mr. Blake doesn't want any of us discussing her, madam. He was most insistent about that."

That fact itself only increased her curiosity. It might make sense if he himself did not want to hear what might be heartbreaking recollections of his late wife. But to forbid the servants to share those memories with anyone else? She could not comprehend it.

"I understand that you must respect my husband's wishes," she said in a conciliating tone. "So must I. He doesn't wish for me to ask anyone about her." She gave the maid a conspiratorial smile. "Of course, that makes me even more curious. And if you would assuage that curiosity, I would certainly never dream of telling him. It wouldn't be good for either one of us."

"That is true." Janet chewed her lower lip and then, impulsively, sat down in the housekeeper's chair. "I wasn't here when the first Mrs. Blake was living, but the stories I heard about her!"

"What sort of stories?"

"Oh, about how she came to marry Mr. Blake when they had only known each other for a few weeks, that sort of thing. And of course there was so much talk after her death."

Cecily felt exultant. This was just what she wanted to hear. "How did she die?" she asked. "Did she have some wasting disease?"

"Nothing like that—it was very sudden. She drowned."

For some reason that surprised her. "On a voyage, do you mean?"

"No. Right here in the bay."

"What? How? Sea bathing, do you mean?" Cecily could not imagine swimming in that bleak, choppy ocean, but perhaps the first Mrs. Blake had been made of sterner stuff.

Janet shook her head. Her eyes were large and avid. She was enjoying herself. "It was a boating accident. She was out with Mr. Blake." She leaned forward and whispered, "I think perhaps he feels a bit guilty and that it was his fault. He won't tolerate discussion of it."

"Well, of course he doesn't wish to discuss it," Cecily said stoutly. "He must have been completely distraught, to lose her so suddenly when he was so devoted to her."

"That isn't what I heard." Janet leaned forward eagerly and lowered her voice to an excited whisper. "I heard that they weren't happy together at all."

"What? Who said that?"

"Someone who was in a position to know, madam. There were arguments. Raised voices. And sometimes they wouldn't speak to each other at all."

"But then..." That changed things dramatically. It threw her entire conception of Connor's first marriage into doubt.

Then she recalled the unfinished letter. It had seemed harmless enough, but still—it meant that Eleanor Blake had been in communication with a man not her husband. Had Connor known about the doctor? And if he felt responsible for her death, did that mean that he actually had borne some responsibility, or just that his conscience was uneasy? Perhaps the guilt was shared—or misplaced. But even after so short a time of being married to him, Cecily knew that if Connor had been jealous of his first wife, if he had suspected she was misbehaving with the doctor, his rage would have been terrible indeed.

"Do you think she did away with herself?" Cecily asked.

Janet gave her a shocked look. "Madam, that is a terrible thing to say. The poor soul was buried in the churchyard right and proper, whatever anyone may think."

Still, if the marriage had been truly unhappy, suicide did not seem out of the question. That might make Connor feel unwarranted guilt. Then a worse suspicion came to Cecily.

"Do people think that it was his fault? That he somehow caused the accident?"

Up until now Janet had been completely frank, Cecily was certain. But now the maid avoided her gaze. "I'm sure no one thinks such a dreadful thing, madam."

But her voice was halfhearted. Before Cecily could frame her next question, Janet rose from the chair, eyes downcast.

"If you'll excuse me, madam, I should be getting back to my duties. Mrs. Ansley will be wondering where I am."

"Of course," Cecily said automatically. "It's time I was going, in any case."

"We can speak again tomorrow, if you wish," Janet promised, though Cecily could tell she was lying. The girl then dipped into a quick curtsey and left the room.

Cecily could not help puzzling over the conversation. Long after she had left the housekeeper's domain and returned to her own, she reflected on what Janet had told her—and what she had refused to say. If the girl could be trusted and the rumors she had repeated carried truth, the marriage must have been unhappy—which went against everything Cecily had observed in Connor's demeanor, going all the way back before they had even spoken to each other, to the time when she knew him only as a sober widower who merely observed rather than participating in whatever entertainment was at hand.

It was possible, of course, that they had had a turbulent marriage but loved each other nonetheless. Or that after his wife's sudden death Connor had repented of their quarrels and grieved for the happiness that might have been theirs if they had been able to get along amicably.

That might especially be the case if he felt responsible for her death. And judging by Janet's sudden reluctance to discuss the matter, it might even be possible that he *had* been responsible. But to what degree? Even if rumor painted her husband as incompetent at best and a murderer at worst, that did not make it fact, or even likely.

All the same, it was food for thought. And unless she gathered the courage to ask Connor herself, rumor and hearsay were all she would have to go on.

Then she shivered as a new realization came to her. If Eleanor Blake's spirit was restless and indeed present in Sterne House, that could mean that she had vengeance in mind. It could mean that her soul would not rest until the man who had caused her death—or failed to prevent it—paid the price.

CHAPTER SIX
Eleanor

Their first visitor at Sterne House was unexpected. Eleanor was in the dreary morning room, trying to compose notes to acknowledge sympathy letters, when the maid announced a Dr. Grant.

The name was strange to her, and Eleanor told the maid to show him in, assuming that he was a neighbor paying his respects in ignorance of her mourning. But there was little respect in his demeanor when he appeared.

"Miss Fairley?" he demanded. "I've come for an explanation."

She stared. "I'm afraid I don't know what you mean."

He gave a short, humorless laugh. He had thick brown hair and a short beard, and features that might have been pleasant if his expression had been less pugnacious. Eleanor put him at a few years older than herself. "I had heard you were a woman of intelligence, but evidently the gossip was mistaken. You know very well why I'm here."

Irritated, she said, "As long as we are pointing out each other's shortcomings, sir, you seem to be ignorant of both my marriage and my bereaved state. My name is Blake now. And I don't know what I have done to deserve the honor of this visit, so pray enlighten me."

"As it happens, I am aware of the tragic death of your father. That is what drove me out to this godforsaken corner of the country to speak to you. I have no doubt that this catastrophe is owing to Mr. Fairley's death and the unhappy fact of your inheriting his responsibilities."

Her temper flared. "By what right do you speak so rudely to me? Just what is it that you blame me for?"

He glared at her. "Why, the discontinuation of construction on the hospital, of course! Did you not recognize my name? I was hired by your father as the first doctor to take up residence there upon its completion. And now I find that not only has work stopped on the building but that no one seems to know just when—or if—it will resume." As she stared in shock, he added cuttingly, "Perhaps it is not a glamorous use for your father's money, but a hospital would do far more good for Surrey than any of the shiny gewgaws you may want to purchase."

"Enough," she snapped. "You must believe that this is the first I have heard of construction having been halted. I had nothing to do with that. Indeed, I share your dismay." She rose and strode past him to the door. "Perhaps my husband can shed some light on the matter."

She led the way to Connor's study and rapped at the door. Connor's voice bade them enter, and Eleanor showed the doctor in.

The contrast between the two men was marked. Though they were probably much the same height, the doctor was more compact and seemed to hum with energy even when he stood still, hands planted on his hips. Connor, instead, sat seemingly at ease, only his eyes flicking over the visitor. He was dressed impeccably in a bottle green suit perfectly tailored to his sturdy form. The doctor wore an old black coat and scuffed, down-at-heel boots, yet he did not look intimidated.

"Is it due to you that construction on the hospital has ceased?" he demanded before Eleanor could perform an introduction.

"It is." Connor's jaw set, and the way he eyed the doctor boded nothing good. "May I ask what business it is of yours?"

"What b—why, I am sworn to look after the health and welfare of those around me. It is entirely my business. Even literally so."

"Ah. You must be Grant." Connor's guarded manner relaxed into boredom. "You should have received a letter informing you that you no longer have a position at the hospital. I am sorry for the inconvenience."

Eleanor stared, aghast. To learn that her husband had halted construction staggered her—and that he was so high-handed with the young doctor shocked her nearly as much.

Dr. Grant gave a short laugh. "The inconvenience to me is as nothing to what the townspeople will endure without a local hospital!"

Connor shrugged. "That's a pity, but there are more urgent uses to which my wife's legacy are being put."

"Such as?" It was the doctor who put the question, but Eleanor was curious about this herself.

"That is our private business. I invite you to cease badgering my wife and catch the first train back to Surrey." When the other man made no move, Connor's face darkened and he rose from his chair. "I think it's time you left, doctor."

The doctor did not seem intimidated. Indeed, at first he looked poised to argue. Then, with a glance at Eleanor, he seemed to change his mind. "Sorry to have troubled you," he muttered, and strode from the room. He shut the door with a bang.

The echoes had not yet died away when Eleanor asked, "What use more urgent than the hospital can there possibly be for my father's money?"

Her husband regarded her in some surprise. He had already resumed his seat and taken up his pen as though nothing had happened. "My dear, wedding tours do not come cheap. Then there is the considerable matter of restoring this house—we cannot have it fall to ruins. Having a new gasworks built to bring proper lighting here will cost a small fortune by itself. And there are other philanthropic enterprises to which your father made commitments. Mr. March detailed all of it for me."

It made sense, of a sort, but it was no less painful. "I think the hospital is more important than Sterne House," she said, but not as firmly as she had intended.

He sighed. "I can see that that eccentric young man's ravings have moved you, but in this matter you must trust to me, Eleanor. I am your husband, and that places the responsibility on me to do the thinking for both of us. Please believe that I do not take that responsibility lightly."

"Of course. But Papa wanted—"

"What of the things you and I want?" he returned, startling her with his irritation. "Don't you wish to have a house you can be proud of, where distinguished guests will feel welcome? Don't you wish to see the drive crowded with the carriages of ambassadors and dukes and generals?"

Momentarily diverted from her point, she said, "Do you mean here, at Sterne House? But I thought we were only to stay for a short time."

With a gesture so sudden that it made her start, he flung his pen away. Drops of ink scattered across the blotter, and he sprang out of his chair and came to stand before her. His height and substantial build, so comforting in other circumstances, were intimidating now, and she had to fight the impulse to back up.

"Sterne House is worth ten of that contemptible hole in Surrey," he said evenly, "and no man of any ambition would confine himself to such a place. Don't you see, a home with some history and grandeur is a requirement for a man in my position. And you yourself will gain in influence as Sterne House becomes known as a place where people of importance gather." His dark eyes held a coldness she had not seen before. "Don't you want that?"

In the face of his displeasure she was close to tears. She did not know how to respond when spoken to this way. Never before had he shown harshness to her, and perhaps that was why she felt as distressed and panicked as though he were attacking her.

"I want the hospital to be built," she said. But her courage failed, and she said it in so meek a voice that it shamed her.

For a moment she feared she had truly enraged him. But then he laughed, not unkindly, and bent to kiss her forehead. "You need an occupation in order to be contented, it seems. But you needn't look to the hospital for that. After all, one of these days we shall be welcoming a tiny Eleanor or Connor into our lives, and I should think being a mother will take up a great deal of your time and interest for the foreseeable future." Taking her by the chin, he smiled down at her. "Don't you agree?"

Delight at the prospect of being a mother flooded her heart, pushing all else aside, and she beamed. "Oh, I hope so. I hope for that so much."

Mollified, he put his arms around her and drew her closer. "I'm glad to know that we are of one mind on that subject, my dear."

Silently she agreed, feeling the rapid frightened beating of her heart gradually slowing against his. But before she could entirely relax once more, he released her.

"Is there anything else you need, Eleanor?" The tenderness had left his face. He might have been addressing a servant.

"N-no," she said in confusion. "That is—not just now." But he had already turned his back and was returning to his desk. Evidently his work was more interesting than she was.

Then she chided herself. She had interrupted him in the first place, after all. It was no wonder if he was testy.

Moving quietly so as not to disturb him, she slipped out of the room and shut the door behind herself. She had started to return to the morning room when through a window she saw Dr. Grant striding down the front path, balled fists shoved into his trouser pockets, the tails of his coat flapping as if in agitation.

Hurrying to the front door, she drew it open, hoping the creaking would not be heard in Connor's study. When the study door remained closed, Eleanor darted down the front stairs.

"Doctor, wait!" she called softly, but he did not turn around. When she had caught up she seized his arm to stop him. He turned a startled face toward her.

"I want to apologize," she said. Realizing she was still gripping his arm, she released it. "Please believe I had no idea what my husband had done regarding the hospital. Had he told me his intention, I would have spoken quite strongly against it."

To her surprise, he took her hand. "I'm glad of this chance to speak to you again, Mrs. Blake," he said in a voice very different from the one he had used before. "I wanted to apologize as well. You did nothing to warrant such rudeness from me. I was thinking about all the people who stood to benefit from the hospital—those who cannot afford to travel to London for care—and my concern made me testy."

"In your shoes I should probably have spoken in much the same manner. It distresses me greatly to think that the inhabitants of Surrey will be deprived of care for their serious ailments."

"Not entirely." There was a determined glint in the young doctor's eyes, which she saw now were a clear and vivid blue. "I have decided to take a house in the area and supplement the services of the local sawbones. But I could do so much more with the resources of a hospital at my command."

Was that a curtain stirring in one of the windows? She hoped Connor was not watching. But even if he was, the matter was too important not to pursue.

"Don't give up hope," she said. "I shall speak to my husband again." With every minute that passed, Connor's anger grew less real to her. She knew now that he needed to be approached differently; she would not make such a mistake again. "I suggest that you put all of your strongest arguments for the hospital in a letter to him, so that he will have all that information at hand when I next bring up the subject. In fact, send me a copy as well. When I am flustered I tend to forget things." And she was so unused to confrontation that she knew she would become flustered again the next time they discussed the hospital.

The doctor shook his head glumly. "It won't do any good. Your husband has clearly made up his mind. He'll not allow himself to be swayed now by either of us." He raked his fingers through his hair, perhaps to assist thought, and a pensive expression came over his face. He looked younger when he was not in a temper, and she could see how he might actually appear attractive under other circumstances. "Perhaps funding could be found from another source," he said in a more optimistic tone. "Some charitable institution or generous benefactor in need of a new project, say."

It was Eleanor's understanding that such bodies always had more claims on their money than they could satisfy and would not be sitting about wondering whom they could lavish their wealth upon, but she did not want to discourage him. And there was a chance he might in fact be able to find a donor. With his passion for the project, he might well sway other philanthropists. So she said, "I hope that success will attend your search, Dr. Grant. Please let me know when you have any news."

With a glance at his surroundings that wordlessly conveyed his distaste for them, he said, "I don't expect to venture to these parts again."

Her own disappointment surprised her. "I may be able to call on you in Surrey," she said. After all, even if Connor did not plan for them to reside at the house in Bridewell Lane, that did not mean she could never visit it. "I still have the house there."

Her visitor's eyebrows rose. "I didn't realize that, Mrs. Blake, though of course I shall be glad to see you if you should come back to Surrey. Gossip has been mistaken before, of course—and I had best remember that, lest I go roaring into another innocent woman's parlor." His grin was so engaging that his earlier temper seemed like something she had only imagined. Then he sobered. "I was remiss before. Permit me to offer my condolences, belated though they are. Your father was a fine man."

"You knew him?"

"Only by reputation. Enough to know that losing him must be very difficult for you."

"It is," she said, and found that she had nothing more to say.

When she did not speak again, he sketched a bow and released her hand, which she had forgotten he was holding. "I'll bid you farewell, then, and leave you in peace," he said. "Wish me luck, Mrs. Blake. I shall need it—and so shall the hospital."

She truly did intend to speak to Connor again about the hospital, but after the doctor's departure her thoughts returned to his cryptic comments about the house in Bridewell Lane. He had seemed to imply that he had heard she and Connor had given it up. Did Connor truly mean for them to live at Sterne House only and never return to Surrey?

Anxiety about raising the subject again made her stomach sink all the way down to her toes, and her mood was so depressed that she was at pains to prevent Connor from observing it that day at luncheon. But she had to know for certain.

She waited until he had taken the edge off his appetite. Then, with her best attempt at nonchalance, she asked, "Do you think we might spend a few weeks at the house in Surrey? It would be more pleasant while all the improvements are being made here. Or if you need to remain here to supervise, perhaps I could go for a short stay."

Connor was sifting through a stack of papers beside his plate. "Oh, the house has already sold," he said almost absently.

Her heart gave a sickening lurch. "Sold?"

"To a button manufacturer and his family, so I believe." When she sat silent, appalled at this knowledge, he looked up. "If you are attached to any of the furnishings or decorations and wish to keep them, I can have March retrieve them before the new owners move in. He is having all of the personal belongings you left behind boxed up to be shipped to us in short order, so an extra knickknack or two shouldn't present a difficulty."

She wanted to plead that the house itself was a personal belonging that she was attached to. All of her memories of her father—indeed, her entire life, her youth, everything that was hers—were bound up in the house on Bridewell Lane. The thought of strangers living there, treading the same floorboards, even using the same furniture, brought tears to her eyes, and she squeezed her eyes shut to force them back. After that glimpse earlier of her husband's capacity for rage, she didn't want to anger him again.

She realized the silence was stretching too long. She must give him an answer. "I can make a short list, if that is all right," she said, managing to keep her voice almost steady. "Pictures, books, that sort of thing."

"Very good. And don't forget to include anything you might wish for our son to inherit one day."

"And the servants?" she ventured.

"What?"

"I told all the servants when Papa died that they would always have a place in my household, and that if they chose to seek employment elsewhere I would give them references."

Connor shrugged. "A pity you made promises you could not keep," he said.

She opened her lips to protest, but he had already turned his attention back to his papers. She wondered now what they were. If he had had her house sold without her knowledge, what other aspects of her future life might at this moment be being decided by a stroke of his pen?

It was a new sensation, and an alarming one, to realize that her life was no longer hers to command. Her father had been indulgent, patient, and generous, susceptible to persuasion and cajoling when necessary. Except for her desire to go to the Crimea, he had never denied her anything she had felt truly strongly about. So she was accustomed to having things more or less her own way—within reason, of course.

But now she was married to a man with a much stronger will and, she was beginning to see, with a definite vision of what he wanted their life to be. Whether or not she had the same vision did not seem to matter to him as much as she had expected.

The next morning after breakfast she decided it would cheer her to consult Mrs. Ansley about a room to be fitted out as a nursery. But when she rang, the maid who answered the summons professed not to know where the housekeeper was.

Not to be so easily thwarted, Eleanor descended to the servants' quarters. She was still unaccustomed to having so large a staff, and the sheer number of people bustling about was almost overwhelming, even though they all stopped what they were doing when they saw her. It did not help that she had not yet learned all of their names.

The butler, whom she recognized by his formal dress and air of authority, approached warily. "I am Furnish, madam. How may I help you?"

Being the focus of so much watchful attention made her self-conscious. "I am looking for Mrs. Ansley," she said.

The butler shifted his feet and did not meet her eye. "I fear she must be otherwise occupied at the moment, madam. May I assist you instead?"

"I'd really prefer to speak to her, Mr. Furnish." When this did not merit a response, she added, "I won't be upset if she had to step away from her post, I assure you. You needn't worry that you'll get her into trouble by telling me where she is." The balding man seemed to relax slightly. "Mrs. Ansley received word a short time ago that her mother-in-law had had a fall, madam. Mrs. Ansley felt compelled to go to her aid and determine how serious the injury was."

"And where does her mother live?" Depending on the answer, the housekeeper might now be a train journey away.

But Mr. Furnish assured her that the housekeeper's mother-in-law lived in the nearby village, so Eleanor returned to her room long enough to don a bonnet, mantle, and walking boots before taking up her medical bag and setting out in pursuit.

As she strode down the rutted lane under an overcast sky, listening to the harsh crying of seagulls, she found that her spirits were lifting despite the cheerless scene. It was more than the beneficial effects of physical exercise, she realized, even though she enjoyed the breeze against her cheek and the warmth imparted to her limbs from vigorous motion. Being away from Sterne House lifted her mood, and solitude in which to pursue her thoughts was welcome.

She was still trying to reconcile herself to the startling revelations of the day before. Sterne House was now her home, a blow from which she was still reeling. Even now she had to fight back tears at the knowledge that this place, which meant nothing but desolation to her, was where she would be forced to reside.

But she must put on a brave face, for the other unwelcome revelation was that her husband would not be tolerant of sulks or defiance. His wishes were now law.

The cold wind cut through her cashmere mantle and made her shiver. Or at least she told herself it was the wind. Altogether she was grateful when she came in view of the cottage she sought and could focus her thoughts on something else.

The housekeeper was astonished to find her at the door. "Mrs. Blake, I do apologize," she exclaimed. "I was so worried when I learned of my mother-in-law's accident that I just up and left. I should have spoken to you first, but I feared...I thought..."

"You were afraid that I would forbid you to go. You needn't have worried."

The housekeeper's apprehensive expression became one of confusion. "Then why are you here, madam?"

Eleanor brandished her medical bag. "I came to see if I can be of any help to your mother-in-law."

Color flushed the other woman's cheeks, and she exclaimed, "That is most kind of you! It would relieve my mind, and that's the honest truth. Will you come through?"

Eleanor followed the housekeeper into a dark, stuffy room largely taken up by a bed. In it an elderly woman lay with one leg propped up on pillows. She regarded the visitor with curiosity if not enthusiasm.

"Mother Ansley, this is Mrs. Blake from Sterne House," the housekeeper said gently. "She has most kindly come to offer her assistance."

"Very kind, I'm sure," said the old lady with a touch of asperity, not surprising in someone in pain, "but it's a doctor I'm needing."

"I am a nurse, Mrs. Ansley," Eleanor said, "and I shall certainly send for a doctor if I find that your injury requires more care than I can provide. May I have a look?"

The old lady gave her assent, and Eleanor seated herself on the edge of the bed. Tending to her ankle was a simple business and took little time. When Eleanor told them it was only a sprain, though a severe one, both the patient and her daughter-in-law were as grateful as if she had done something superhuman. After making certain to open up the sickroom windows to permit fresh air—and leaving strict instructions not to shut them except in case of rain—Eleanor and her housekeeper walked back to Sterne House. The journey was much different from the outward one.

Mrs. Ansley proved to be a pleasant conversationalist now that she felt more at ease with her mistress. Although she proved reticent about the topic of her late husband, she was more forthcoming about her early years as a maid at Sterne House and her knowledge of the grounds. Nor did her knowledge of the surroundings stop there. As they were crossing the shore, she pointed out places where she and her friends had played as children.

"There were caves where we played Ali Baba," she recalled. "We had to be careful not to be there when high tide came, though—at least with some."

"Weren't you frightened of drowning?"

"Goodness, no, madam. We could all swim. We were in and out of the sea every day that the weather was warm enough. But we learned to be careful. You see there, the darker stretch of water, almost like a path?"

Eleanor saw a swathe of slate blue in the lighter surface of the ocean that surrounded it; she seemed to remember its being that way even in her childhood. "A riptide," she said.

"It can be dangerous if you get caught in it and don't know what to do," Mrs. Ansley continued. "It is quite safe, though, if you let yourself be carried by it down to the cove. But there, you're hardly likely to be bathing on such a bleak and lonely stretch of beach. I only know about it because my sisters and I used to look for oysters to eat. With so large a family, we had to find our meals where we could." Then she darted a guilty look at Eleanor. "Which is not to say, madam, that the late master was ungenerous."

"I should be astonished to learn otherwise," Eleanor said mildly. "My memories of my grandfather are not rose-tinted, I assure you." As they approached the house, she said, "Mrs. Ansley, I don't wish to make your position in the house difficult—or mine, I must admit. I believe my husband prefers for me to remain on more formal terms with the staff. I trust you will not mind keeping this episode to yourself?"

"Of course not, madam," the housekeeper exclaimed. "I would never wish to cause you any inconvenience."

"Thank you. I'll go ahead, then, shall I, and you can follow a bit more slowly?"

"As you wish, of course, madam."

Eleanor quickened her strides. She had a feeling that her husband would be ill pleased if he should learn of this adventure, and she was thinking about how to ensure that old Mrs. Ansley received care during her recuperation. She dared not make a habit of these solitary excursions into the village, or at least not without a pretext that her husband would condone.

That evening, having been unable to come up with such a pretext, she composed a letter to Dr. Grant. "I know you are kept quite busy attending to your patients in Surrey," she wrote in part, "and I have no wish to divide you from them. But it would be a kindness in you to designate some nurse or assistant to travel here to Norfolk and visit Mrs. Ansley from time to time to examine her ankle, re-bandage it, and watch for complications. I will of course arrange for payment."

The predicament of old Mrs. Ansley was soon pushed to the back of her mind, however.

Connor's behavior toward her began to change. She told herself that this was probably the quite natural progression of a marriage once the honeymoon was over, but she grieved nonetheless over the growing distance between them. He had less time for her, and although he seemed eager for them both to make social connections, when he invited guests to the house he seemed embarrassed by her presence.

"You look like a crow" was his blunt statement on one such occasion.

She tried not to take the remark personally, but she could not help feeling injured. "I'm still in mourning, Connor."

"You could at least set aside your weeds when we have guests. That black dress makes you look at least fifty years old. Why don't you wear the purple satin with the black trim? You'll still be in mourning colors."

She did not point out that, while purple was worn during half mourning, her loss was still far too recent, and in any case satin was decidedly too shiny for the purpose. Instead she wore the gown to dinner that night, along with some of the jewelry Connor had given her, and tried to be more animated at table.

Nonetheless, she saw him glancing from her to the vivacious young Mrs. Lavery, clearly dissatisfied with the contrast between the guest's youth and fair-haired beauty and the very different picture Eleanor presented.

Though he insisted that he desired a child, he came to her bed less and less frequently. Most nights he slept in his dressing room or even on the divan in his study. His temper was short, and he became so disagreeable at times, so cutting and sarcastic, that Eleanor took to slipping silently out of a room when she heard him approaching.

She became adept at deception, so much so that it surprised her. She sent letters under cover of mail from the housekeeper. She learned to pretend to her husband and the servants that she was contented with her life at Sterne House.

But the greatest deception was one she practiced upon herself—when she tried to pretend that she had not begun to fear her own husband.

CHAPTER SEVEN
Cecily

Cecily's life at Sterne House began to pall more quickly than she would have dreamed possible.

At first, to be sure, it was a pleasure and relief not to have to sing for her supper, as it were—to be always amusing or useful. Here, in her own home, she could relax. She could even be lazy. She could spend her days frivolously trying on every single beautiful gown she owned or writing boastful letters she would never send to old acquaintances who had behaved badly toward her. She could, and did, spend hours reading the opening pages of random books in the library in hopes of finding one that would seize her interest.

But in fact she found herself chafing at the lack of useful occupation. Connor encouraged her to learn to ride, but although she liked the idea of going hacking with her husband—and imagined she would look very fetching in a riding habit—she found that she and horses shared a mutual wariness and that she greatly preferred to keep her distance from them. She had no desire to expand upon her meager talents at the piano or singing. She had no acquaintance in the area to call upon or invite to call; Connor was the one who issued invitations.

As for his own company, he was frequently occupied with matters pertaining to the estate, its maintenance and refurbishment. More and more often she chose to soothe her loneliness and fretful mood with a lavish tea, and she realized that if she continued to indulge herself so, her beautiful new wardrobe would no longer fit.

Worse than the boredom, though, was the eerie sense of being watched. She could never predict when or where she would feel it. Sometimes it felt as though weeks passed when she was free of it. At other times it seemed to come more than once a day. There was no particular room in which it manifested itself, so she had no way of avoiding it. The morning room, the parlor, the dining room, the library—it was always the same: the feeling of her scalp tightening and her muscles tensing as she felt, almost tangibly, some invisible watcher's gaze upon her. Her eyes would dart about in search of some human cause, and she listened with all her strength, but never could she find any normal explanation.

The gloominess of the house only made her more nervous. She was eager for the gaslight installation to be completed, but the work kept encountering unexpected delays. One rainy morning when she was listlessly sketching a vase of flowers a commotion came to her ears, and she found a group of workmen arguing in the corridor.

"I tell you the tools was all here," one was saying. "Yesterday evening I laid them all out ready for us."

"Well, they ain't here now, are they?" another retorted. "Someone must've walked off with 'em."

"Who would do such a thing? None of us would be fool enough to think we could hide it. And that ain't all. Look at the glass shades, all shattered and broken! We'll have to send away for more."

Intrigued, Cecily drew closer. The men were clumped near what she realized was the first Mrs. Blake's door. They weren't just confused and frustrated—they were actually frightened. She remembered that they had come to Connor when they had experienced similar mishaps before.

"Is something wrong?" she asked, and startled faces turned toward her.

The one who seemed to be in charge straightened and gestured to the others to remove their caps. "I hope we haven't disturbed you, Mrs. Blake," he said in a different voice.

"Not at all. If someone is deliberately sabotaging your work, my husband would wish to know of it."

The man tried to shrug away the idea, but his eyes did not meet hers. "Now, ma'am, there's no need for that. We've just—had a few delays, like."

One of the other men muttered, just loudly enough to reach her ears, "A few!"

"This is not the first time such a thing has happened, is it?" Cecily pressed. "Your tools have been stolen or damaged before."

Suddenly all the men were talking.

"It's happening more often now."

"The scaffolding was broken when we tried to paint."

"The paint was emptied onto the floor."

Cecily lifted a hand to quiet them so that she could be heard. "Is this all taking place in one part of the house?" she asked.

The leader, who had given up trying to keep the matter quiet, shook his head vigorously. "Different rooms, mum. But not everywhere. And we weren't bothered when we were working out in the grounds."

So it was only indoors. That would seem to indicate one of the house servants. Surely an outside party would have been observed entering or leaving upon one of these destructive errands.

"And you've no idea who is doing all of this?" she asked.

Now the men were not as eager to speak. They ducked their heads so they would not have to meet her eye. Finally the eldest of the men, whose beard was gray and who looked as though he could be the father of most of the others, cleared his throat.

"Begging your pardon, missus, but we've heard as the last lady of the house left it sudden-like, and young," he said. "In my day I've seen some queer things, and all of our troubles and delays seem to me like the lady's spirit ain't at rest."

Cecily felt an uneasy prickling at the back of her neck. Was the first Mrs. Blake angry at attempts to change the house her spirit still claimed as hers?

"What makes you think so?" she asked. "I'm not doubting you, mind—I'd simply like to know what led you to that idea."

He gave her a look as though he was gauging whether she was going to laugh at him. Evidently he was convinced of her sincerity, for he said, "For a start, every now and then we get to feeling as if we're being watched."

Cecily gasped before she could stop herself, and that seemed to encourage him to continue.

"The feeling was strongest in the lady's bedroom, though at one time or another we've all sensed it. There are strange noises—"

"Rats," scoffed another.

"When have you seen a rat in this house, I ask you?" the older man retorted. "There ain't none. Besides, no amount of rats would take our tools." Turning to Cecily, he added, "We've not told any of this to Mr. Blake, seeing as we don't want to lose this job like the others."

"But what do you tell him when he asks why your work isn't progressing faster?"

The gray-haired man gave a rueful chuckle and rubbed the back of his neck. Cecily was starting to like him. "Well, missus, we've been a bit tongue-tied, and that's a fact."

She could well imagine. Though she had never tried to discuss the supernatural with Connor, she could picture him being quite withering on the subject. Still, now that she was not the only one to have experienced strange things in the house, perhaps it was worth risking his scorn and determining if he knew of an explanation.

But bringing up the subject of his late wife ought to be a last resort, since it would be painful for him. If only Mrs. Ansley would unbend enough to speak to her frankly! She probably knew better than anyone the inner workings and secrets of Sterne House.

"Would you like me to speak to him on your behalf?" she offered, and instantly realized it had been the wrong thing to say. From the sudden coldness radiating from them, she guessed that the men resented her intrusion into their realm and had no desire for a woman to do their speaking for them.

"That's right kind of you, missus," the man in charge said without warmth. "We couldn't put you to that trouble, though. Now we'd best be getting on with our work, seeing as Mr. Blake is relying on us to make the house fine for you." He gave a nod of both thanks and dismissal.

Dispirited, she retreated to the morning room. She would have liked to know what Connor would have said had the workmen taken their suspicions to him.

Unexpectedly, she found herself in a position to learn this the next night at the evening meal. It began when, in all innocence, she had asked her husband what he had been up to that afternoon.

"Writing to March," he told her. "I need him to find new workmen to install the gas lighting."

"What happened to the ones who were here already?" she asked, and was saddened but not surprised when he said he had dismissed them.

"Superstitious bunglers, the lot of them. Lagging behind in their work, and when I asked why—a reasonable question, I would have thought—they came up with some cock-and-bull story about an evil supernatural presence in the house."

Now that she had an opening to bring up the topic, she felt she had no choice but to make use of it. But she could not deny that she was apprehensive about it.

"Do you believe in ghosts?" she asked.

Connor put down his fork. The rain of the day before had only worsened, and now a storm was rising; even through the heavy damask curtains she could hear the shrill voice of the wind.

"Ghosts?" he repeated. "Of course not. A foolish superstition."

She bit her lip. "Are you quite certain? Because I think... that is, I believe that we have one. Here at Sterne House."

He stared at her and gave a short laugh of disbelief.

"You believe the same codswallop as those benighted rustics? Nonsense. Even if ghouls existed, why should Sterne House would be haunted?"

As much as she had wished to avoid it, it seemed she was going to have to make her meaning explicit. She only hoped the subject would not cause him great pain. Carefully she said, "Some people say that the souls of those who have died prematurely, or tragically, linger in the places they inhabited in life."

His hand, in the act of raising his wine glass, halted midway to his mouth. "Ah," he said. "Eleanor."

"Do you think her spirit might be restless?" she ventured. She could not tell whether he was angry, grief-stricken, or neither. His dark eyes were unreadable.

"I would prefer," he said quietly, "not to speak about her."

"I'm sorry, Connor. It's only that—haven't you felt it yourself? This nagging sense of being watched?"

"I am happy to say I haven't. Eleanor is already too much in my thoughts."

"So you don't think she could be...haunting us?"

He placed the wine glass on the table before him and began to twirl the crystal stem between his fingers, gazing at it as intently as if it held the answers to all life's questions. "Eleanor drowned," he said. "It was a terrible accident, but it was all over very quickly. I don't believe that she suffered."

Her momentary feeling of relief was shattered when he continued, "I can't say the same for myself, however. To watch my wife sink into the ocean and be swept away from me before I could so much as say her name. Then the desperate searching. Lanterns on the water, shouting for her over and over. Dawn arriving with no success. Days of agony, knowing she must be dead but clinging to hope. Perhaps she had made her way to land far away, injured, unable to ask for help to come back to me."

"Connor, I'm so sorry—"

"And then her body washed up a week later, battered and swollen, her face half eaten away, her dress torn to shreds by the force of the waves and the rocks." His voice had grown harsh, and she forced herself to stay silent. She had opened up the memory of hell before him, and now he was staring it down. "Good God, it was a sight I shall carry with me for the rest of my days. My lovely bride, drowned and decayed."

Tears sprang to her eyes. Never would she forgive herself for putting him through this. Springing up from her chair, she went to kneel by him and take his hand in both of hers. "Forgive me, love," she said. "It was thoughtless and cruel of me. Please, please don't dwell on her." She reached up to stroke his face. "Tell me what I can do to make things right."

Slowly, as though he were coming to the surface after a trance or a nightmare, he turned his head to look at her. The smile he gave her was faint and painful, but at least it was a smile.

"Don't reproach yourself," he said. "You are young, sweetheart, and will learn soon enough what wounds cannot bear to be reopened." Reaching down, he lifted her to sit on his lap. "Come, kiss me, and all will be forgiven."

Filled with penitence and pity, she kissed him over and over, willing the pain to leave him as if the force of her love and determination could heal his heart.

It was a relief to her in many ways when Connor became more pressing in his desire for children. There was a solution to nearly all of their problems. Connor's heartache would vanish in the face of a baby, and as for Cecily, at last she had something to do.

Her days were increasingly taken up with preparations—poring over furnishings for the nursery; selecting fabrics and wallpapers with the housekeeper; sewing all of the dresses for the infant. Or rather, since her sewing was poor, choosing patterns and having Mrs. Ansley locate seamstresses to do it for her.

The prospect of having a baby neither frightened nor delighted her. She had not spent a great deal of time around children and had only general impressions of them, formed by the different families who had hosted her over the years. Generally, she was aware, a nursemaid and then a governess or tutor would do the greatest part of the work of raising the little one, and she as the mother would have only the enjoyable parts. Then, before she knew it, the baby would be a fine young man setting out for school or a sweet young woman ready to marry and begin the process anew.

A child would be good for Connor. He could be so moody, so darkly forbidding, that sometimes she was afraid to approach him. Yes, with a baby in the house, someone to carry on his name, he could not help but be more pleased with the world—and with his wife. And what beautiful babies they would have! Their children could scarcely help but be the loveliest babies in the world, with two such parents.

As the weeks passed and Cecily did not find herself expecting, despite what could only be described as dedicated effort on her and her husband's part, she became uneasy. She had no mother or married female relative to tell her whether this was normal. Cousin Margaret, a spinster, was scarcely an authority on these matters. Perhaps she should consult a doctor.

In fact, perhaps she should consult this Dr. Grant that her predecessor had tried to communicate with. It would be an exciting opportunity to fill in some of that picture. Learning whether he was shifty or high-handed or honest would help her understand her husband's first wife a bit more.

She had never shown the unfinished letter she had found in the writing desk to Mrs. Ansley, and she decided it was high time to do so. Perhaps the housekeeper could cast some light on it and at the very least identify the writer definitely.

But when she went to open the drawer of the writing desk, she saw that the contents had been disturbed. It was nearly empty now, and there was no sign of the letter to Dr. Grant. Vexed, she shut the drawer once more, remembering the eerie feeling of having been observed that day for the first time. Was it possible that something had in fact been watching her—and had gone after her and removed the letter?

If that was the case, it certainly suggested that this Dr. Grant bore some importance.

When she decided to approach the housekeeper about the matter, she took care to do so one morning when Connor was well out of the way, overseeing something to do with the improvements in the grounds.

"Do you know a Dr. Grant?" she asked Mrs. Ansley at luncheon. "Particularly one close by?"

She thought there was an instant's pause before the other woman said, "No, Mrs. Blake. I'm not familiar with a doctor by that name."

Janet, who was clearing Connor's place at the table, straightened with a surprised expression. "But, Mrs. Ansley—"

The housekeeper fixed her with a steely eye, and the girl subsided, reddening.

"As I said, madam," the housekeeper said. "There is no Dr. Grant in this part of the country."

"I see," said Cecily, whose curiosity had been piqued to such a degree that she could scarcely refrain from commanding the housekeeper to tell her the truth. As it was, she managed to wait until she had an opportunity to speak privately to Janet.

"You know of a doctor by that name, don't you?" she asked. "Mrs. Ansley just wouldn't let you say so."

Janet nodded, glancing all about to make certain they were alone. "He just moved into the village a few months ago—around the time that you came to Sterne House, in fact, madam. So it is possible that Mrs. Ansley simply doesn't know about him."

Cecily shook her head. The housekeeper had been far too emphatic in silencing the maid for that to be the case. She was not the sort of woman who would prevent lower servants from correcting her simply to save face, at least not when the wishes of the master or mistress were paramount. She knew something.

But what? Why would this man be important enough to lie about? It made Cecily think that her earlier theory might be true: the doctor and Eleanor Blake might have been engaged in some underhanded business, and the housekeeper might be protecting the first Mrs. Blake's reputation...or perhaps she even feared that the man might corrupt Cecily herself if given the chance.

"What is he like?" she asked.

"I'm afraid I've never met him, madam," Janet said, to her disappointment. "I could send for him, if you like."

"Oh, that isn't necessary." The idea almost made her panic. Heaven knew what Connor would think if he found this man in his house—the one with whom he had forbidden his wife to correspond, as far as Cecily knew. "But if you could find an address for him, without letting anyone know it was I who asked, I would very much appreciate it."

Janet's eyes brightened, and her chest swelled with self-importance. "I surely will, madam! You may rely on me."

"Thank you," said Cecily, now perversely filled with uncertainty. If only she could be certain the girl would keep the matter secret.

This was far from the only secret at Sterne House, though; indeed, they seemed to flourish within those cold stone walls. One day when Cecily had a sneezing fit and stepped into her husband's dressing room to fetch a handkerchief, since she was nearer to it than her own, she found a yellowed piece of paper in his top bureau drawer.

It was not a letter, like the one that had mysteriously vanished from the morning room. Rather, it seemed to have been torn from an old ledger. A small snippet of fabric was attached to it, a faded cotton in a pattern of blue blossoms on a dun background, as one might have seen in a dress worn by a woman of the serving classes.

There was writing in a delicate hand, faded to a rusty brown by age. It read:

> *James Snow, baby boy, aged 3 months; son of Laura Snow, spinster (26), of West Riding. Admitted 15 June 1823.*

She was gazing at it, trying to puzzle out what it meant, when a heavy tread announced her husband's arrival. Then the paper was snatched from her hand.

"What are you doing snooping amongst my things?"

She had never seen Connor so angry. Patches of red were burning on his cheekbones, and he loomed over her, so intimidating in his height and size that she shrank from him.

"I was just fetching a handkerchief," she said in confusion.

"So you thought you would invade my privacy and search among my belongings?" He shook the paper in her face. "I suppose you can't wait to tell everyone about this."

"I just happened upon it! I don't even know what it means."

"A likely story."

A spark of indignation came to her rescue. "I swear to you, Connor, I've no idea what that paper signifies. All I desired was a handkerchief, and your dressing room was close by."

Slightly mollified, he tossed the paper back into the drawer and pushed it shut. "I'm sorry I frightened you," he said at length. "It's only that that is private, something I cannot share even with you." He forced a smile. "Can you forgive your grumpy husband for being such a brute?"

"Of course," she said, as she knew he meant her to, but the image of him looming over her in rage was one that lingered in her mind long afterward.

As was the mystery of the strange names. James Snow... who could he be? And what was he to Connor?

Still later, another question came to her. If Connor was so anxious to keep the paper's contents secret, why did he not have the thing hidden in a place more secure? He had a safe in his study. It would have been easy enough to conceal it there, where he need never worry about anyone stumbling upon it.

But her next thought only added to her perplexity. Was the document's meaning, whatever it was, so significant to him that he needed to keep it within arm's reach?

Though minor in itself, the incident served to show Cecily something very important: that she did not in fact know the man she had married very well at all.

CHAPTER EIGHT
Eleanor

"I should like to go into the village today," Eleanor said to Connor at breakfast one day in late October.

Her husband did not look up from the papers he was examining. "The village?" he repeated.

"I feel I ought to call on old Mrs. Ansley and see how she's faring." When he frowned, she prompted his memory. "The housekeeper's mother-in-law. I bandaged up her sprained ankle some time ago."

"Why should you need to return, if it was only a sprain?"

Because I want to get away from this house, even if it is just for an hour. "Because it was a severe sprain, and there is a risk of complications. Besides, although I know we aren't quite in the role of landlords, I feel we owe something to our neighbors."

He looked up from his papers at last, and she felt a nasty little jolt at the coldness of his dark eyes when they met hers. He weighed her words for a moment. "I don't like the idea of your going by yourself. Take Mrs. Ansley with you."

"I'm quite safe on my own," she said. "I should hate to take her away from her work."

"Seeing to your needs *is* her work. I'll not have you gadding about by yourself. Anything might happen."

"Very well. I shall ask one of the maids to accompany me."

His lips thinned as though she was wearing on his patience. "That would be taking her away from *her* work, Eleanor. In any case, I'm sure Mrs. Ansley would welcome the chance to visit her mother and see to her condition."

His insistence was having the effect of making her more stubborn. Even though she knew it was unwise to cross him, it felt as though she never got to follow her own desires anymore, even in so small a matter as a walk.

"It isn't very far," she ventured. "I don't see why I cannot go alone."

He gave a grunt of displeasure. "Out of the question."

She dropped her eyes. Her heart was thudding beneath her ribs as it always did when she felt they were in opposition, and she struggled to keep her voice even. "I know you don't mean to, Connor, but when you ask something like this it makes me feel as though you don't trust me."

His fist came down on the table, making the silverware jump. Eleanor jumped as well. But his voice was terribly quiet when he said, "Eleanor, I believe I am a reasonable man. What possible cause have I given you to be so resistant to a simple wish like this? Any number of hazards could lie in wait for a woman unaccompanied. You speak as though I suspect that you plan to rendezvous with a secret lover and run away together. Believe me"—witheringly—"that is the last thing I would expect."

Eleanor saw that her hands were shaking and clasped them in her lap. She felt dangerously close to tears and had to take a few breaths to master the feeling.

"I'm sorry, Connor. I suppose I do sound unreasonable."

"Then milady will consent to her husband's humble request?"

The sarcasm lashed her, and she flinched. "Of course," she said, almost inaudibly.

He pushed away from the table and went to yank the bell pull. "Well, thank heaven for that."

She sat in silence, hating herself as always for not knowing the right thing to say to prevent such scenes. Surely other women knew how to cajole their husbands into granting small requests, like a solitary walk. Yet here she was, provoking her own into a rage and seemingly unable to prevent a simple discussion from becoming an argument.

When the maid named Mildred appeared at the summons of the bell, Connor pointed at Eleanor without looking at her. "Your mistress will be taking a walk and requires Mrs. Ansley to accompany her. Be so good as to inform her—and see that my wife has her mantle and whatever paraphernalia she requires."

When Eleanor did at last leave the house and set out for the village, accompanied by the housekeeper and carrying her medical bag and a bunch of flowers, her heart lifted. It mattered not that the day was overcast and the wind raw; she breathed more easily simply being out of Sterne House and, she was forced to admit, away from her husband.

"I hope you don't mind my taking you away from your work," she said to the housekeeper.

"It's kind of you to grant me the opportunity to visit my mother-in-law," Mrs. Ansley said, but this was no more than what she would be expected to say to keep her position.

"You needn't pretend it isn't inconvenient to be dragged away with no warning," Eleanor told her. "It is only that my husband insisted upon it."

The other woman darted a quick look at her. She was carrying a lidded pot filled with broth and wrapped in a linen cloth. "Then I am doubly pleased that I may be of use to you," she said. "Keeping one's husband in countenance can sometimes be a challenge, in my experience—though naturally the master is a far more distinguished gentleman than my late husband."

Eleanor did not reply. Belated anger was beginning to rise in her, warming her cheeks and making her walk so quickly that her companion had to exert herself to keep up. Why did this anger never come to her rescue when she needed it, when she was actually facing her husband? The humiliating truth was that when he spoke to her with sarcasm or contempt, she felt only wounded, sick, and hurt. She could not defend herself in those moments. Only later, when she was away from him, did she think of the arguments she could have marshalled or recognize how she could have defended herself against his barbed words.

She was distracted from these unhappy thoughts when they arrived at the cottage and found that old Mrs. Ansley, still bedridden, was being tended to by a girl from the village and a young, bearded man whom Eleanor did not at first recognize.

"Mrs. Blake," he said. "What a pleasure to see you."

It took her a moment to place him, and he must have noted her confusion, for he laughed. "After our first meeting, I must be difficult to recognize when I'm not in a temper," he said. "I hope to make a better impression on you this time."

"Nonsense," she said automatically, extending her hand for Dr. Grant to shake. Seeing him again made her realize that her memory of him had not been quite accurate. Or perhaps it was indeed seeing him in a good humor that made her realize he was quite a handsome man. His glossy brown hair was combed straight back to reveal a high forehead, and his short brown beard framed a mouth that seemed always ready to smile. His bright blue eyes had endearing crinkles at the corners as though from much laughing, and his eyelashes, unusually long for a man, gave him an ingenuous look.

Surprisingly, he truly did seem pleased to see her. Faced with his warm expression, it occurred to her that her husband had not smiled at her in what felt like a long time.

"I thought to see how Mrs. Ansley is faring," she said, placing the flowers on a side table, "but now I feel my presence is superfluous."

Old Mrs. Ansley held out her hand to Eleanor. "Dr. Grant has been taking excellent care of me, but it is always lovely to see you, my dear." Then she gave a chuckle. Her soft round face was creased in smiles, and she drew Eleanor close enough to speak into her ear. "I declare that having a handsome doctor is the best cure!" she said in a loud whisper.

That made Eleanor smile. "I shouldn't wonder."

Dr. Grant took the old lady's wrist in one hand to feel her pulse. "Mrs. Ansley is my best patient," he said affectionately. "She is always in fine spirits, which does nearly as much good as any medicine." To his patient he added, "Now, you are wonderfully improved, but I want you to continue taking these drops nonetheless. Better safe than sorry, don't you agree?"

How warm and reassuring his voice was when he spoke to the old lady, and how well he combined authority with gentleness. Eleanor was not at all surprised when Mrs. Ansley agreed to follow all of his instructions.

"Perhaps I ought to leave," Eleanor said. "I'm sure you and Mrs. Ansley need to discuss her mother-in-law's condition."

"On the contrary," said the housekeeper briskly. "Now that you have seen to your patient, doctor, I would enjoy the chance to sit with my mother-in-law a bit." To the village girl she added, "Be a good girl and make some tea for the doctor and Mrs. Blake. I'll give Mother Ansley some warm broth."

Before she realized it, Eleanor and the doctor were settled in the tiny front room of the cottage with tea, and he was telling her anecdotes about the more amusing side of his practice. The anger and frustration she had seen in him on their first meeting were almost vanished, except when he spoke of patients whose needs he was unable to meet because of lack of resources.

Eleanor's cheeks burned at the recognition of all that her failure to underwrite the hospital meant, but when she tried to apologize, the doctor was quick to excuse her.

"It's none of your doing, Mrs. Blake. No doubt you are doing as much good here in this backwater as the hospital would do if your father's plans had gone through."

"Hardly," Eleanor said, too ashamed to look at him. "To tell the truth, I find that my life here is quite different from what I would have hoped."

Her change of mood did not go unnoticed. Setting his teacup aside, he leaned forward in his chair. "Is everything well with you, Mrs. Blake?"

The easy charm had been replaced by a more serious mien, and his eyes were so earnest and sympathetic as they looked into hers that she lowered her gaze.

"Everything is fine," she said, and cast about for another topic. "I confess I am surprised to see you here, Dr. Grant, since you have not sent me a bill for your services."

Now he looked confused. "I did," he said. "Two, in fact. This is far from my first visit to Mrs. Ansley. While I find her company delightful, I had not intended for them to be merely social calls. Did you not receive them?" When she shook her head, he said only, "Perhaps the bills were lost."

That was just his being tactful. "Both of them?" she said. "No, something is amiss. I shall ask—that is, I shall see what I can find out."

The silence after her words made her burn with embarrassment. She could imagine what was running through his mind. A wife too cowardly to ask her husband about a small matter of money. A husband who dismissed legitimate bills his wife incurred. When she made herself look at him, she expected to see pity at best, contempt at worst, in his eyes.

Instead what she saw, and it made her throat constrict with unshed tears, was plain, friendly sympathy. He took her hands in his, and even through her gloves she felt the reassuring warmth of his touch.

"Mrs. Blake," he said, "is there any way in which I can help you? Forgive my frankness, but you seem more troubled than when we first met. I was concerned when I never heard from you, and now I am more worried than ever."

"I never wanted to live here," she blurted before she realized she even meant to say it. "All I wanted was to build the hospital and help keep it running. To look after people who needed it. But ever since Papa's death, everything feels out of my hands." Until that moment she had not put her feelings into words, but they came rushing out as if straight from her heart. She realized, with a shock, that she was able to speak more freely with this relative stranger than with her own husband. "I never thought of myself as an ineffectual person," she said, "but that seems to be what I have become. And I hate it! I don't want to be such a—a limp noodle!"

His laugh comforted her. It was somehow companionable. He said, "Even though I haven't known you for long, ma'am, I can say with certainty that you are not that." He released her hands to produce a handkerchief, which he handed to her. "But I can understand your feelings of frustration."

She blew her nose and wiped her eyes. "You aren't telling me that this is a wife's lot in life and that I must reconcile myself to what my husband desires," she said.

His mouth quirked wryly. "Such platitudes aren't usually very helpful," he said. "And I think you are more resourceful than that. But whenever you are in Surrey, you may always call upon me if I can be of help in any way."

"You are very kind," she said, "but I fear that I—"

Over the doctor's shoulder she saw the bedroom door open, and she fell silent.

The doctor turned to see what had caught her attention, then rose. "Ah, Mrs. Ansley. Is your mother-in-law resting well?"

Mrs. Ansley nodded, putting a finger to her lips, and Eleanor wondered how much she had overheard. "She has gone to sleep," she said softly.

"It is the best thing for her," Dr. Grant said. "I shall look in again in a few days' time."

"We can't thank you enough, doctor."

When he smiled at the housekeeper he looked almost boyish. "Your mother-in-law is one of my favorite patients, ma'am. Naturally I wish to keep a close eye on her. And I hope Mrs. Blake will continue to as well."

"I shall do my best," Eleanor said. Considering how difficult Connor had been with regard to this visit, she was afraid to make promises she could not keep. She thought the doctor gave her a considering look, but he said nothing until the three stood outside preparing to go their separate ways.

"If you do have the opportunity to see that Mrs. Ansley continues taking her drops, I should be grateful," he said to them both generally. "My work in Surrey does not always allow me to travel here."

Eleanor's face burned, and she fumbled to unclasp the seed-pearl brooch at her throat. "We have taken advantage of your generosity quite enough, doctor," she said, thrusting the brooch at him. "Please take this in payment for your attendance on Mrs. Ansley."

"But, Mrs. Blake—"

"I know that a doctor cannot afford for his bills to go unpaid. It would make my conscience easier if you took this."

With the laughter fallen away from his face, he looked older and almost stern. Slowly he said, "If you wish it, ma'am. Thank you." Then he tipped his hat to both women and said, "Farewell, ladies. I hope we shall met again."

Miserably Eleanor watched him go. Had she wrecked the fragile friendship that had just begun to form? Perhaps he thought her patronizing, playing at Lady Bountiful, when all she had wanted was not to take advantage of him. Silently she and Mrs. Ansley started back to Sterne House as the doctor strode briskly in the opposite direction. Eleanor glanced back over her shoulder once, but he did not look back.

The housekeeper's voice startled her, coming as it did out of a silence. "Mrs. Blake," she said, "I must tell you something. Your husband has asked me to inform him of all your movements and plans."

This was not much of a shock, considering their earlier conversation. "Did you agree?" Eleanor asked, and the other woman hesitated.

"I need this position," she said. "It allows me to be close to Mother Ansley and to pay for her keep. But you have been so kind, and spying on you would feel shabby."

Eleanor reflected on this. "Do you know whether any of the other servants have been asked as well?"

"I don't know for certain. Perhaps Mr. Furnish."

That would make sense. The butler was able to move about the house more freely than any other servant except for Mrs. Ansley herself, and Eleanor could not envision her husband stooping so low as to converse with the maids and footmen.

She was still musing when Mrs. Ansley said, "You needn't worry that I'll tell him that we encountered the doctor today, of course."

"No, you should," Eleanor said. "My husband must feel that he can trust you to be my warden. If he believes that your loyalty is with him, that may make life easier for both you and me."

After a quick, surprised glance, the housekeeper gave a nod. "If you think it best, madam."

Dinner that night passed largely in silence, as it so frequently did. Connor read the newspaper as he ate, giving Eleanor the opportunity for much reflection on many things—Dr. Grant and his kindness chief among them. Watching her husband, she observed that his mouth, though beautiful, had a cruel quality to it, at least in contrast with the doctor's. Of course, that might have been her knowledge of her husband's propensities coloring her perceptions, but there was a strong physical difference between them quite apart from the difference between their characters.

While the footman was holding the platter of fish so that she could serve herself, Mrs. Ansley entered the room and went directly to Connor's chair. She spoke quietly to him for a few moments, after which he dismissed her. When the door had closed behind her, Connor touched his napkin to his mouth and said, "I am informed that you had a rendez-vous with Dr. Grant in the village."

Startled at the falsehood, she let her fork drop, and the clatter was jarring in the quiet room. "There was no pre-arrangement," she said. "He was attending to old Mrs. Ansley. It was mere chance that Mrs. Ansley and I arrived during his call."

Her husband's dark, hooded eyes were cold. "Do you truly expect me to believe that? When you gave the fellow your pearl brooch?"

Her stomach felt hollow. She had not been prepared for the housekeeper to mention that. "I gave that to him in pay-ment for his medical services," she said, but she did not dare look at him as she said it. "He said he had sent bills to us that have gone unpaid. I would not have the man starve."

With a scoffing sound, Connor pushed his plate away. "That hardly seems likely. Men of his sort can always sepa-rate foolish women from their money."

Of his sort? As though he were some kind of confidence man instead of a member of a respected profession! Anger parted her lips, but she was prevented from speaking as her husband went on. "It is an ugly thing when a man finds that he cannot trust his wife. You have only yourself to thank, Eleanor, so don't try to play on my feelings as you did this morning. You have made it clear that you cannot be left by yourself."

A chill seemed to seep through Eleanor's limbs. "You mean I cannot go to the village anymore?"

"Not alone. From now on, whenever you leave the house, Mrs. Ansley shall accompany you." He gave her a tight, humorless smile. "Of course, as you yourself observed, you will be taking her away from her duties on these occasions. So I suggest that you not leave Sterne House more than is absolutely necessary."

Her scheme had gone badly awry. If only Mrs. Ansley had not embroidered the truth to put her in the wrong! Or had she told Connor no more than the truth, only for him to misconstrue it? That was probably more likely. Whichever was the case, the outcome was worse than Eleanor had bargained for. Now she was little better than a prisoner. Attempting to keep her voice even and reasonable, she said, "Surely I am too tame to require a chaperone. If you'll give me another chance—"

"We'll not have this discussion again, Eleanor. You will respect my wishes as your husband."

He returned to his newspaper, holding it up like a barrier to further conversation. He might as well have shut a door in her face.

Rebuffed, she looked at the scar on his hand and remembered the day when she had stitched up that wound. That had been the beginning of everything. Did he ever regret the mishap that had brought them together?

Or had it been a mishap at all? For the first time she wondered if he had purposely cut himself as a pretext for getting close to wealthy Lemuel Fairley's daughter.

"Connor," she said, making her voice as mild as possible, "was it really an accident when you injured your hand at the hospital building site?"

He made her wait for a reply, as she wondered in dread whether she had touched off his anger again. But his voice, when it came from behind the newspaper, was curiously mild.

"If it was deliberate," he said, "it was a small enough price to pay for getting to be on friendly terms with an heiress."

It was as good as an admission. She felt sickened at the realization of how he had deceived her...and by the horrifying other possibility that now seemed to present itself. She took a breath and tried to sound as cool as he had, though her heart thudded at her audacity.

"And my father's death? Was that an accident?"

This time he lowered the newspaper to look at her. She braced herself for his rage, but none came.

"My dear Eleanor," he said softly, "one wonders how you could bring yourself to marry me if you truly thought me capable of cold-blooded murder."

Until that moment she had not really believed it. But he was so composed. They sat staring at each other, as Eleanor heard her breaths coming ever faster and more shallow, when running footsteps approached and Mildred the maid threw open the door. At the same time, a clanging bell began to sound from somewhere outside the house.

"Begging your pardon, sir, madam," said the breathless maid, "but there's been an accident."

"What accident?" Connor said in irritation. "What is that infernal noise?"

Eleanor knew, but she let the girl tell him. "A ship has foundered, sir. It's in a bad way."

"Well, what do you want me to do about it?"

"We can send out boats," Eleanor said. "We must try to rescue as many as we can." She stood, making her husband stare at her.

"You don't imagine that you can do anything, do you?"

"Some of the survivors will probably have wounds that need tending to, probably even broken limbs," she said. "I may be able to help. Shall we give the order to send out boats?"

She had a feeling that he would have refused out of sheer obstinacy had the maid and footman not been present. As it was, he gave a curt nod.

Mildred asked, "Will you be manning one of the boats, sir?"

Connor gave a grudging assent. In this matter Eleanor did not blame him for his reluctance. She knew, though he did not, just what a grim situation was awaiting them. This was far from the first wounded ship to go aground in the shifting, treacherous bay.

The scene that was unfolding when they reached the shore was the stuff of nightmares. The screams of those trapped aboard the ship were echoed by those in the water, flailing to keep afloat until one of the boats could reach them. She knew that some of the boats were embarked now not in order to rescue people but to salvage what they could from the ship. The lantern lights on the boats shone on anguished faces—and calculating ones. And over all came the din of the bell, unceasing.

Connor's face went still with shock as he took it in. Then he said, "You may come out in the boat with me, if you like."

She shook her head. "I shall do better on land."

She meant that she would be of greater use there, but he misunderstood.

"Of all the times to indulge a fear of the water," he snapped, then motioned William the footman to follow him to the boat that was readied for him. Soon it was afloat, and he and the men servants busied themselves hauling exhausted men from the water into the boat.

Eleanor stood on the shore with her medical supplies and a store of blankets and clean bandages. Two of the maids had build a driftwood fire over which a kettle was constantly replenished with a warm cider, liberally dosed with spirits. Many of the survivors needed little more than warmth, internal and external, to set them aright, but there were bruises, scrapes, and gashes, and one broken arm, which would need to be seen to by a doctor as soon as possible.

When her husband returned to dry land, his face was changed. "It's hellish out there," he said, taking a mug of hot cider from one of the maids. "I've never seen the like."

Eleanor considered that a strange thing for a soldier to say. But then she told herself that fighting in a battle, no matter how violent and gruesome, was different from the situation in which they now found themselves. "Do you think many remain to be saved?" she asked.

"I imagine not. Some of the boats have left already—I suppose they've given up."

Or else they wanted to hide what they had salvaged in one of the caverns along the shore. Before the month was out Eleanor suspected many of the village houses would be sporting improvements that bore a striking similarity to the goods transported on that ship.

By dawn it was agreed that there were no more survivors to be rescued. For days afterward, the crippled ship rested slantwise in the bay, remained as a sobering reminder of the havoc and tragedy that could erupt in just moments from a shifting of the ground invisible below the surface.

After that night they both seemed to avoid each other. Eleanor was haunted by the memory that he had not denied murdering her father. The idea of Connor deliberately crushing her father's skull was too horrible to bear, yet she must not dismiss it. After all, Eleanor herself had spoken of the dangers of the work site in Connor's hearing. It was not too great a stretch of the imagination that he had taken inspiration from her words. And if he was capable of that ruthless violence against her father, what might Eleanor now expect him to do when he had wearied of her?

In her efforts to avoid him, she found an unexpected resource.

Her grandfather had liked to frighten her with tales of secret passages and hidden chambers used by the wreckers of old for hiding their booty and evading capture. Now that she was grown, Eleanor assumed those tales were simply invented. But one day she made an unexpected discovery.

The interior of the house was of a much more recent vintage than the exterior, which was not surprising; some former owner, no doubt wearying of dark Tudor decoration, had had new paneling put up. But the rooms had a symmetry that was at odds with the structure of the house, and here and there were odd little makeshifts that might have been created to make the new interior fit. The doorway between parlor and entry hall, for example, was so deep it was nearly a hallway. And when Eleanor once observed a manservant hammering a new nail into the paneling of the morning room, the sound was oddly hollow. Was there space behind the wall?

Since Connor was occupying himself elsewhere, as had become his custom, Eleanor took advantage of the solitude to examine these areas more closely. To her fascination, she found that in the dining room there were narrow doors hidden in the paneling that admitted her into the space between the new walls and the old. When she ventured into one of these spaces, hiking her crinoline up on one side to fit into the narrow dimensions, she found that although it was dark and stuffy, cracks between the panels and occasional peepholes admitted some light.

The peepholes suggested that the hidden spaces had been adopted for servants' use at some point. Indeed, it was silly to think of these hidden byways as secret passages at all. But Eleanor still felt a thrill at being able to move unseen between and behind many of the rooms. It took her back to her childhood days, only this was even better, since there was no frightening grandfather to scare her with ghost stories.

On her first venture she did not go far, merely past the parlor and her husband's study. The only people she saw were two maids, engaged in a dull conversation about cleaning the lamp chimneys.

The second time she went exploring behind the walls was a dull, rainy day. She knew Connor would be meeting with the landscape architect to discuss yet more plans for the grounds, so she planned to bypass his study and see if she could access the library. Connor disliked it when she expressed the intention of going there, saying that she would strain her eyes and begin to squint, so she preferred that he not know she went there at all.

But it was the sound of his voice that halted her on her dark, dusty journey.

"My wife," he was saying, "simply doesn't come into the matter."

She stopped short. There was a crack of light just ahead, and she went up and put her eye to it.

Her husband was seated behind his desk, leaning back in his chair with a cigar in one hand. The pungent smoke irritated her nose, and she held her breath for a moment so that she would not sneeze. In the chair on the other side of the desk from Connor sat a white-whiskered man who was unrolling a sheaf of diagrams—the landscaper, no doubt.

"You know best, of course, sir," he said. "But as an old married man, I can tell you that wives have a way of making life unpleasant when they don't get a say. For instance, might Mrs. Blake raise a fuss about taking out these flower beds here?"

Connor said, "Mrs. Blake's wishes are moot. I am the one who makes the decisions in this household." The older man was quick to change tack, evidently eager to maintain harmony between them. "To be sure, the ladies are always trying to insert themselves into matters where they don't belong."

"Exactly." Setting the cigar aside, Connor leaned forward to examine the plans. "Besides," he added, "she will not be with me for much longer."

"Ah, is she departing on a journey? Or is it something more serious? I hope it isn't an illness."

Connor raised his head. His dark eyes gazed into the distance, but they were fixed on a spot on the wall close to Eleanor's peephole, and she shut her eyes for a moment lest some glint of light reflect off her eye and betray her presence.

"It is," he said, almost absentmindedly. "An illness that I fear will prove fatal."

Eleanor felt a cold wave wash over her.

The older man started to voice condolences, but her husband waved them away. "I have had time to resign myself to my inevitable loss," he said. "I knew when we married that her health was fragile. But if it is the will of Providence, there is nothing to be done."

"Such a tragedy," the other man said, with the matter-of-fact air of one who had lived through many of them. "But with all of the improvements you are making to Sterne House, I hope you not leave it deprived of a mistress—the jewel in its crown, so to speak."

Connor's gentle smile struck a sickening, hollow feeling into the pit of Eleanor's stomach. "Believe me," he said, "Sterne House will not go long without an ornament worthy of its grandeur."

Feeling faint, Eleanor leaned against the stone wall behind her, and the cold seeped into her body through her clothes. Without that support she might not have been able to continue standing. When she recovered enough to move, she fumbled her way back toward the morning room, and the sounds of the two men conversing faded away behind her.

When she reached the morning room, she sat down until she could stop shaking, which was not for some time. As shocking as it was, she had no choice but to believe that her husband intended to rid himself of her.

That night she observed him drinking more heavily at dinner than was his usual habit. She wondered with some trepidation if he was seeking courage for some reason, but she said nothing. By now she knew better than to remark upon any behavior of his, for he would take it as a criticism.

They parted to retire as had become their custom, and Eleanor was secretly relieved not to have him as her bedfellow. He had been so frighteningly remote that evening, even as his face reddened and his gestures grew looser with every glass of spirits.

She fell asleep easily but woke, with disorienting abruptness, some time during the night. The door of her bedroom was open to Connor's dressing room, and a dark figure was silhouetted there.

As she watched, it began to advance toward her, slowly and silently. It had to be Connor...but there was something so strange about this stealthy approach toward her bed. He lurched once but caught himself, and he did not stop until he loomed over her.

She had not made a move or a sound. She was beginning to be frightened. Perhaps, if he thought she was sleeping, he might go away...and then she would lock her door.

She could hear him breathing heavily, as though with effort. Why did he not speak? Her pulse thudded in her ears as he raised his arms, and she saw that he held a pillow in his hands. He began to bring it close to her face.

She could picture it pressing it down so that she could not breathe, and in a burst of alarm she exclaimed, "Connor? What are you doing?"

At once he drew the pillow back and fell back a pace. "Eleanor?"

His voice was slurred, but it sounded almost as horrified as hers had.

"What is it?" she said.

One hand went to rub his face. From the other the pillow dangled. She stared at it in dread.

"I thought you were asleep," he said at length.

She shivered.

"No," she said. "Not quite." He said nothing, and she ventured, "Why don't we talk in the morning, Connor? I think you ought to get some rest."

After what felt like years he nodded. "Good night," he mumbled, and turned to go.

It was agony waiting for him to make his way out of the room. When he was finally out of sight she darted up from the bed and across the room, where she shut the door swiftly but as quietly as she could. This time she locked it.

She could not go back to bed, though. Could not forget how agonizingly helpless she had felt lying there as he advanced with the pillow. And she knew with a terrible certainty that if she had in fact been asleep when he approached, if she had not startled him and struck some doubt or dread into his heart, her husband would have smothered her to death.

Although Connor did not make any more blatant attempts upon her life, she found herself constantly doubting the safety of ordinary things. She could not look at a cup of tea without wondering if it contained poison, could not walk down a flight of stairs without envisioning herself tumbling down them and breaking her neck if a carpet rod had been removed. She hoped that Mrs. Ansley was doing what she could to keep her safe, but she could not know for certain—and there were limits to what a housekeeper could do.

One windy night in early March there came again the sound of the bell announcing that a ship had gone aground. Eleanor, reading alone in the library, started up. She must fetch her medical bag, which had seen little use since the last disaster.

In the corridor she was met by Connor and the housekeeper.

"I expect you will be going out on the boat with Mr. Blake," the housekeeper said to her. "Mildred is fetching your oilskin mantle."

"I'd rather not go out on the water," Eleanor said. "The sea is so rough. I can be of greater help on the shore."

Connor glared. "Your place is with me," he told her. "Besides, you will be able to tend to the wounded more quickly."

Mildred came at a run with Eleanor's waterproof mantle, and Mrs. Ansley handed a lantern to Connor.

"If you'll forgive me for saying so, Mrs. Blake," she said, "I think this is a time to overpower your fear. Surely you will help your husband most by remaining at his side."

"Exactly," Connor said. "Come, Eleanor. There is no time to argue."

She opened her lips to protest again, but his face was set and determined. "Very well," she said.

It seemed that little time elapsed before she was seated in the boat, holding the lantern, while her husband pushed the prow into the choppy sea, wading out into the dark water until it nearly reached his chest. The surface of the water was churning, the air filled with the toll of the bell and the cries of both those in danger and their rescuers. It was chaos wherever Eleanor looked.

The boat was afloat now. Gripping the side with both hands, Connor pushed up out of the water and over the side, which rocked so wildly that Eleanor was propelled from her seat.

The lantern slipped from her hands and crashed to the bottom of the boat. The oil flared upward in a sudden flame, and Eleanor was thrown over the side and into the water. Before Connor could cry out or speak a word, she had vanished beneath the surface of the sea.

CHAPTER NINE
Cecily

As autumn waned, Cecily felt the chill touch of winter come to Sterne House—and her marriage.

It was gradual at first. Connor's remarks about desiring children went from hopeful to sour. She sometimes found him frowning at her, most often when she had been laughing over some small jest or absorbed in a magazine that he found insufficiently elevated. But the clear turning point was the visit of Viscount Longhurst, his wife, and their daughter, the Honorable Augusta Norris.

Connor said when they arrived for their stay that he particularly wanted to show Sterne House at its best, and Cecily planned to do her best to make her husband proud. But when he saw her the first night in the gown she had chosen for dinner, he frowned. "I doubt whether the viscountess dresses in pink gauze," he said. "Something with a bit more grandeur would have been preferable."

"Ah, but it wouldn't do if she and I were dressed the same," Cecily said teasingly.

Her response did nothing to ameliorate his mood. "Lady Longhurst and her daughter are held to be paragons of fashion," he said. "You would do well to pay close attention to what they are wearing and learn from it."

"You always used to like me in this dress," she said, surprised and wounded. "You said it made you think of an apple blossom."

He adjusted his tie in her mirror. "Apple blossoms are little better than weeds next to a perfect rose."

Sure enough, at dinner he was most attentive to Lady Longhurst and her daughter, Augusta. The girl was around Cecily's age, no more than nineteen, with a cloud of dark hair and a perfect complexion. Her gown, Cecily had to admit, was exceedingly handsome: champagne-colored silk satin embroidered with shining golden flowers. She was not exactly pretty, but despite her youth she had a regal quality that seemed to attract Connor's attention. So did the discussion of her impending engagement to a young baron.

"It isn't entirely decided upon," her mother allowed. Lady Longhurst was on the thin side, with intelligent dark eyes and an aquiline nose. She wore poppy-red velvet with ecru lace. "We don't want to rush into anything, of course."

"So far the young man looks to be all that he claims to be," said Lord Longhurst. He was gruff, not as much of a conversationalist as his wife, and saved his enthusiasm for the saddle of beef.

His wife explained, "One cannot be too careful these days. We are having him fully vetted. If he proves to be all that he promises, we shall announce the engagement next month."

"So soon?" Connor asked, and gave Augusta Norris a smile. "Is he as handsome as all that, Miss Norris?"

A becoming blush stained the young woman's pale face, but otherwise her poise was undisturbed. "The eagerness is my parents', Mr. Blake," she said in a low, gentle voice. "Naturally I will do as they wish."

"It's a pity the lad doesn't have more money," her father said, sawing off a bite of beef. "None of these youngsters seem to be prepared to support a wife. But Augusta is dead set against marrying a man thirty years her senior—more's the pity."

This was said with affection, and the young woman's answering smile was loving. "I don't think that is terribly unreasonable," she said. She looked at Cecily. "It seems to me that you and your husband are very well matched, and you are not so very far apart in age."

"Not very," Cecily said to be polite, though she did not consider a difference of around fifteen years to be a small one. Nor did she mention that her desperate circumstances had not permitted her to exercise any preference about a prospective husband's age.

Connor motioned for the footman to replenish their wine. "Then what is the age you consider ideal, Miss Norris?" he asked. "Would a man of my years suit you?"

The girl's blush deepened. "Why, Mr. Blake, I do not know your age. But I am certain that your wife is fortunate to be—ah—your wife."

Not a great wit, then, but that did not seem to dampen Connor's admiration of her. "Ours is not as grand a marriage as yours will be," he said, "since Cecily has no noble lineage, and my only distinction is my war record. This scar is just one of my souvenirs." He flexed his left hand with a gently wry expression.

What was the point of his effort to charm the young woman? If he wanted a mistress, an eligible young debutante would be the worst possible choice. A safely married peeress would pose far less dangerous potential for scandal or familial fury. Yet he was not flirting in the same way with Lady Longhurst. What did he hope to gain by ingratiating himself with the daughter?

She tried to convince herself that he was merely trying to better himself socially, that she was imagining any deeper design, but her suspicions were only strengthened the following morning.

After breakfast Connor led them all on a tour of the grounds, showing off all the improvements and describing what new ones would be made. Cecily had heard him describe all of these things ad nauseam and fought to keep her smile from slipping off her face as he talked. Even in sunlight the crenelated castle towers still managed to look brutal and threatening, and she found it difficult to understand how the guests could rhapsodize over it.

"Tell me, Mr. Blake," said Lady Longhurst, after having duly complimented the view, "what is that peculiar structure at the bottom of this great pit?"

Connor's chest swelled. He was wildly proud of this particular venture.

"The pit will become an artificial lake," he said. "It will set off the approach to Sterne House beautifully, don't you think? And once the lake is full, the structure you see now will be invisible—from the surface." He gave Miss Norris a roguish grin. "What do you think it is, Miss Norris?"

"Gracious, Mr. Blake, I could hardly venture a guess."

"Some kind of cold storage?" Lord Longhurst offered. "An ice house?"

In his enthusiasm Connor looked more dashing, more like the man Cecily remembered from her honeymoon. It was a pity that her presence could no longer evoke this side of him.

"A ballroom," he pronounced, like a magician conjuring up a trick. "An underwater ballroom. Can't you picture it? Narrow concrete passages lead from the house into a dome of glass. My guests can look up as they dance and see the face of the moon, rippling through the water. Curious fish will swim up to the glass to stare at the dancers. I don't think I'm boasting to say that there has never been anything like it."

"Why, Mr. Blake!" The young woman looked impressed. "What an extraordinary feat!"

"You must have a ball to christen it," Lady Longhurst said, and Cecily could see the idea seize her husband.

"What a brilliant idea," he pronounced. "A ball there shall be, and you must all attend."

"Perhaps a masquerade," Miss Norris suggested. "I do love a masked ball."

"You must have it in March," her mother added, "before the Season begins. After that, everyone will be in the city...and of course Augusta will find herself busy with many social engagements."

"I think a ball would be better in the summer," Cecily said. At that time of year, with the long twilight that lasted for hours, she could imagine dancing beneath the lake with soft pearly light glimmering through the water, revealing the fish flitting around the glass dome. Besides, she knew for a fact that the lake and ballroom would not be completed until July.

So she was astonished when her husband recklessly declared, "As Miss Norris wishes, so it shall be. Ladies, start planning your costumes now, and make plans to return to Sterne House in March for the gala event of the year!"

Cecily watched in disbelief as the four of them chattered excitedly about the scheme. There was something peculiar about the way Lady Longhurst and her daughter regarded Connor, with a kind of proprietary air. Even Lord Longhurst seemed to have forgotten Cecily's presence.

A little cold shiver danced up her spine. Somehow this spelled trouble.

Later she tried to bring it up with Connor. She dressed for dinner with unusual speed and went to knock on his dressing-room door. "Come in," he called idly, and she found him nearly ready, with his valet tying his white tie. He looked surprised but untroubled to see her.

"Connor, is it possible to safely complete the lake and ballroom as early as March?" she asked without preamble.

He regarded himself in the mirror. He was still a fine-looking man, with his strong features and intense dark eyes. His generous mouth curled in a satisfied smile. "Anything is possible with sufficient motivation," he said, almost idly, "and money is a great motivator."

"But when it is something so new—I should think one would want to allow extra time, if anything, to make certain that it's safe."

His valet finished his tie and stepped back. Connor turned to Cecily. "Sterne House was meant to be a showplace. If I cannot make it into something worthy of the Blake name, I have failed. I want everyone in England to speak of it with awe and delight in their voice, to clamor to be invited here. I want my home to be legendary."

My home, Cecily noted. Not *our* home.

"What qualities are you seeking for Sterne House's mistress?" she asked. "I do hope I am up to snuff."

Her tart words seemed to startle him out of a reverie, and the look he gave her was far from reassuring.

"For a start," he said, "somewhat less sarcasm would be more attractive. You had nothing when we first met, as you yourself were at pains to point out to me, and now you are the mistress of a grand estate. For the life of me I cannot understand why you would be anything other than thrilled with your position."

How did he always manage to make her feel that she had put a foot wrong? Confused, she said, "I don't mean to suggest that I'm not sensible of my good fortune, Connor. Only sometimes I feel as though you don't think I am worthy of it."

He relented, to her relief. "You have all the beauty and charm one could ask for in a wife, my dear," he said. Offering her his arm, he found a smile for her, but his dark eyes still seemed to dwell inward on his thoughts. "Come, let's go in," he said, and they made their way to join their guests in silence.

Watching him throughout the meal, Cecily saw how again and again his eyes turned toward Augusta Norris, resting with approval on her elegant coiffure, her regal velvet gown, her dignified posture and bearing.

Cecily could think of only one reason he was behaving this way. He was thinking about marrying again.

He wanted a wife like Augusta. Not even for his own delight—but for Sterne House.

It was toward the end of Viscount Longhurst's family's visit that Cecily began to understand the danger she was in.

Connor had proposed another turn in the grounds, where work was continuing apace on the ballroom. Cecily had noticed that work done in the grounds tended to go more smoothly than the indoor improvements, without the delays caused by the mysterious invisible presence. There had been rain in the night, and while some men might have acknowledged that that made conditions too wet to continue work unabated, Connor was not the man to be hindered in such a way.

"Be careful, ladies," he said as he offered Miss Norris his arm. "The grass is slippery."

Lord Longhurst observed that Cecily was walking unaccompanied and made as though to offer her his arm, but his wife seized it before Cecily could move.

Her cheeks burned. Clearly Lady Longhurst had observed what Connor had made all too clear: that Cecily merited little consideration when Miss Norris was present.

Rebuffed, she toiled along in the rear, holding up her skirts to prevent the wet grass from ruining them, as her husband led them along the edge of the pit, now muddy, where the domed ballroom was taking shape at the bottom. There were a great many pointy edges and metal bars where the foundations were being filled in.

"The next project," Connor was saying, "will be to have the east tower repaired. Even from here you can see that the stonework along the top is in disrepair." He pointed, and the guests dutifully looked. Cecily had never heard him mention this particular project before, but he did not confide everything in her these days. This gave her a little pang, and no small degree of indignation, until she felt his elbow gently nudging her arm.

Her heart lifted. So he was not going to neglect her on this walk after all! Then, as the pressure persisted and grew, she realized in confusion that he was not trying to signal to her to take his arm. He was pushing her.

As the thought took form, she tried to steady herself, but her shoes slipped on the wet grass. With a last sharp shove, he sent her over the edge of the pit.

She dropped without a sound louder than a gasp. Her fingers sought a hold in the muddy earth, but without success. She was sliding faster than she could see or think.

"Cecily, be careful!" came Connor's shout from above.

Cold, clammy confusion, every moment expecting to strike against something sharp. Then she was halted with a jerk.

She realized that she had come to a stop partway down the sloping side of the pit. Head downward, she saw workers start toward her, upside down. Finally she was able to crane her head and see what had happened.

It appeared that the lowest hoop of her crinoline had snagged on some protrusion, perhaps a tree root. When she raised her gaze a little higher she saw Connor and the Longhursts gathered at the edge of the excavation, with expressions of concern ranging from mild to extreme. Connor looked half mad with anxiety. She had never realized before how good he was at pretense.

But though his face and manner showed nothing but concern, his eyes were cold. She had no choice but to see that her very existence was an inconvenience to him, and the realization chilled her more than her tumble into the muddy pit.

"Cecily, dearest!" he called. "Are you all right? I wasn't quick enough to catch you when you lost your balance."

She said nothing. Two workmen came to help her to her feet while a third disentangled her crinoline from the impediment that might have saved her life. Another brought his coat to wrap around her. She was nearly covered in mud, and when she began to shiver she wasn't certain if it was from the cold or the shock.

Her husband continued to reproach himself bitterly. All she could think about was his elbow, pressing against her with greater and greater force until the sudden jab that had sent her over the edge.

"Just a moment, and I shall come down to you," he called out now, and she forced herself to smile.

"Please don't, my love; you'll become as muddy as I am. I'm perfectly fine." She was proud of how normal her voice sounded.

"Truly?" he asked, and she could have sworn she heard disappointment in the word.

"Perhaps a bit shaken and bruised, but no more. I think I shall go in and have a bath." *And hope that you won't come to drown me in it,* she added silently. "Please, all of you, don't let my mishap put an end to your walk."

To her relief Connor did not press the issue. She didn't know what she might do or say if he came close to her again just now. With what she hoped was a carefree-looking wave of farewell, she let one of the workers support her on the slippery walk back into the house.

Once inside she thanked him and sent him away. She could walk well enough, she found, and with some instinct to retreat to shelter she hurried back to her bedroom. There she rang for a maid with the intention of asking her to draw a bath, but it was Mrs. Ansley who answered the summons.

Cecily was already unfastening her mud-stained dress, feeling a strange revulsion toward it, as though it now carried the taint of danger. The housekeeper went to help her, which was startling.

"I am sorry to hear of your accident, madam," she said. "It is a great relief to see that you sustained no serious injury."

"Thank you. I do think it would be best if I could bathe in some Epsom salts, though. And perhaps we have some arnica in the house in case I should start to bruise." She could already feel burning aches settle into her body.

"Of course," the housekeeper said, but she said it absently. "May I suggest another course, though? Janet told me that you asked her for an address for Dr. Grant, and I have been able to locate him. Paying a visit to his office might do you a great deal of good."

Cecily stared. "But you claimed you had never heard of a Dr. Grant."

Mrs. Ansley met her eyes without the slightest trace of shame. "My memory played me false," she said. "Learning of your accident just now helped me to remember."

This was so clearly a lie that Cecily had no idea at first how to respond. Then, her curiosity growing greater every moment, she asked, "Why can't Dr. Grant call on me here?"

"There is bad blood between him and the master, I am sad to say. But it is worth making the trip to see the doctor. He is a trustworthy man, and I'm certain he will be able to cast some light on your situation." She brought a clean dress from the wardrobe and presented it to her. "Shall I have the carriage brought round for you?"

By this point Cecily was tired of feeling manipulated. She was prepared to dig in her heels. "Mrs. Ansley, can you please be more open with me? Why exactly do you wish for me to rush out and see this man whom my husband abhors? If seeing him is worth risking Mr. Blake's displeasure, I need to know more."

The housekeeper's carefully neutral expression gave way for just a moment, and she spoke her next words in a very low voice.

"Accidents tend to happen to the mistresses of Sterne House," she said. "If you tell the doctor about this one, he may be able to help you prevent any more of them."

Now Cecily's curiosity was roused indeed. It actually sounded as though Mrs. Ansley was hinting that the death of the first Mrs. Blake was deliberate. Did she believe that Connor had killed her?

And might it even be true? Cecily did not find the prospect as remote as she would have even the day before.

If Dr. Grant held answers to any of her questions, she wanted to know. "Very well," she said. "But what can I tell my husband if he asks about my taking the carriage?"

"I shall say I sent it round to the doctor's, which is no more than the truth." Mrs. Ansley surprised her with a conspiratorial smile. "He does not need to know *which* doctor, or that you were in the carriage. And I believe Parnell the coachman can be induced to keep our secret. But it is best that you hurry, madam."

Dr. Grant's office was on the ground floor of a lodging house. An elderly and very deaf lady who was tending to the flower bed pointed Cecily to a door beside which was a shingle bearing the doctor's name. When she knocked, a woman's voice bade her enter.

Inside, the office was empty except for a dark-haired woman in an apron who was arranging instruments on a tray. Although too thin for beauty, she had a sweet smile—though it vanished from her face once she saw Cecily fully.

"I'm here to see Dr. Grant," Cecily said, wondering what in her appearance had startled the woman so. "Is he in?"

"I'll just fetch him," the dark-haired woman said almost inaudibly, and darted through the door to an adjoining room. As Cecily waited, she heard low voices in conversation.

Then a handsome man with candid blue eyes, nut-brown hair, and a short beard entered—not at all whom she had pictured, but a pleasant surprise. He definitely showed none of the furtive, shady qualities her imagination had ascribed to him, but neither did he seem the kind of lothario who might tempt virtuous wives away from the strait and narrow.

He looked, rather, like someone one could confide in, someone one could trust. Perhaps that had been his appeal to Eleanor Blake. Neither a co-conspirator nor a partner in illicit activities—just a friend and confidant.

"Mrs. Blake," he said, with an easy smile that settled her last doubts. "Delighted to meet you. I'm Dr. Grant."

"Did I say something wrong to your maid?" she asked, extending her hand to shake his. "She vanished so quickly."

"Mrs. Jones is my nurse. She was just a bit surprised to see the mistress of Sterne House paying a call on me. Now, how may I help you?" He gestured for her to be seated, but when he sat down opposite her he seemed restless, smoothing down his waistcoat needlessly. He kept glancing toward the room in which he had left Mrs. Jones.

Apart from that he was so very normal, so different from anything Mrs. Ansley had prepared her for, that she hardly knew how to answer. Had the housekeeper been mistaken? Perhaps this man had nothing more to offer her than medical expertise.

"Can we speak in confidence?" she asked.

"Of course. Nothing you tell me shall leave this office."

It should have reassured her, but she still did not know how to start. She might as well begin with the plain facts of why she was there. "My housekeeper, Mrs. Ansley, suggested that I call on you," she said. "She is worried about me."

The doctor's expression sharpened into interest. "Worried about what in particular?"

"I had a kind of accident."

"Not a serious one, I hope." He eyed her more closely, probably looking for signs of injury.

"Not really. She suggested I speak to you because—because it might have been serious, under other circumstances." She had to force out the next words. "My husband was involved."

He looked grave but not surprised. "Do you think your husband poses a threat to you?" he asked.

There was no skepticism in his manner, but all the same she wished she had not chosen to come here. When the question was spoken in so many words, even in as serious tone as the doctor's, it sounded far too dramatic and as if she were clamoring for attention.

But at the same time, remembering Connor's cold eyes staring down at her from above the edge of the pit, she felt a renewed dart of anxiety. She knew it had been no accident. If her crinoline had not saved her, she might have been seriously injured, or worse.

The doctor, waiting patiently for her to respond, seemed to understand her discomfort. "Would you find it easier to speak to another woman about this?" he asked. "I can ask Mrs. Jones to step in. She may be able to understand better than I can."

She smiled in relief. As understanding as the doctor seemed to be, he could not comprehend the difficulty of Cecily's situation the way another woman could. Moreover, as a married woman, Mrs. Jones might have some experience of a difficult or even dangerous husband, though of course Cecily hoped that was not the case.

She said, "Thank you, that would be helpful."

The doctor stepped into the next room to summon the nurse, an action of which Cecily approved; she hated it when men simply sat and bellowed when they wanted someone. When he returned he was accompanied by the dark-haired woman, and the looks they exchanged suggested that they were wrestling with some important matter Cecily was not acquainted with.

The doctor drew up another chair, and Mrs. Jones cleared her throat and seated herself. "Mrs. Blake," she said, in a pleasant, low voice that betrayed a thread of tension, "before you say anything else I want to be honest with you."

"Of course," Cecily said, mystified.

Mrs. Jones seemed to have a difficult time finding her next words, and the young doctor, his blue eyes gravely attentive, placed a hand on her shoulder as though to reassure her.

She gave him a quick look of gratitude and then released a long breath, which seemed to calm her. Her large gray eyes met Cecily's steadily as she said, "You would know me as the first Mrs. Blake. I am Eleanor."

CHAPTER TEN
Eleanor

Dying was the best thing Eleanor had ever done. For nearly two years she had been working as a nurse for Dr. Robert Grant. Under the alias Mrs. Jones, she had a modest but useful life, doing work she found fascinating and worthwhile, learning from him and learning also how to be herself again, free of the crushing dread of her husband. The first time Rob Grant had made her laugh out loud, without fear, she knew she had been born anew.

Rob and Mrs. Ansley had helped with the details of her escape, but the plan had sprung into her mind that first night that Connor went out with the boats to rescue survivors of the foundered ship.

"I knew that he was planning to be rid of me," she said to Cecily now, remembering that terrible day when she had been the unintentional eavesdropper on his conversation in the study—and the still more terrible night when he had approached her bed with murder in his heart. "My greatest fear was that he would succeed before I could get away."

"But not just that," said the younger woman, her interest seized. "You went so far as to convince him, and everybody, that you were dead." She had accepted Eleanor's identity at once but seemed to be hungry for every detail of her story.

"Otherwise she wouldn't have been safe," the doctor put in. "He would have pursued her had she only vanished."

"But how did you manage it?" Cecily exclaimed. Her eyes were wide with fascination and, Eleanor thought, some admiration. "And there was a body, wasn't there?"

Eleanor nodded. "I really owe it all to her. Winifred Jones. She was an indigent in an advanced stage of consumption, whom Rob—Dr. Grant—was treating."

"I noticed that there was a resemblance between her and Eleanor," he said. "Not enough to deceive anyone under normal circumstances, but if the body were to be in the water for a week or two before it was found—"

"Yes, yes, I see." Cecily clearly did not want to hear about this portion of the story in detail, and Eleanor took pity on her.

"The first thing was to make certain I had what I needed upon my disappearance. With the help of Mrs. Ansley I was able to spirit some things out of the house and into a hiding place: jewelry, my few valuables, what little money Connor would permit me to have. But I could not take anything whose absence he would notice. And for the escape itself, Mrs. Ansley hid all that I would need in one of the caves opening out of the bay."

"So that you could change into dry things after you supposedly drowned," Cecily marveled. "But how did you manage that? You needed a night when a ship came to grief, and that could not be planned, surely."

Rob Grant grinned. "You'd be surprised what a big enough bribe can do," he said, but Eleanor gave him a rebuking look.

"We did not cause the wreck, of course," she said. "And waiting for a ship to encounter trouble in our bay was nerve wracking, I admit." She thought of those weeks when she had been paralyzed with the fear that at any minute her husband would throw her down a set of stairs or put poison in her food or smother her with a pillow. It had been agony to wait. "In truth, if it had gone on much longer, I would have had to find some other pretense to take to a boat with him. I probably would have had to do it in daytime, however, which was obviously less desirable for my purposes. Or I could have developed a passion for sea bathing, but again, that would not have been as effective."

"It also depended on poor Winifred," Rob added. "We knew her death was imminent, but naturally I could not predict it to the day. And without being able to dress her body as Eleanor, we knew we would come to grief eventually. Some day, someone would see Eleanor alive and well and recognize her, and she would have to return to her marriage—no matter that she knew it would be fatal."

The young woman's face grew thoughtful. Perhaps she was reflecting on her own position. "You were taking a great risk, even so. Why, he might have drowned you just moments before you could swim away."

"That is why I didn't wait for him to get into the boat with me. By making my own choice of when to fall overboard, I had some control over what happened. I knew that if I could find the riptide it would take me to the stone outcroppings, where I would be safe. The shoreline is so uneven there and has so many stone formations that it was fairly easy to remain unseen as I made my way to the caves."

She permitted herself a small shudder, remembering how her sodden clothing had dragged at her like an anchor when she hauled herself out of the water and across the sand and shale. She had thought her heart would burst with the exertion and fear until she finally made her way deep enough into the cavern to know she was invisible.

Then, fearing a light would be seen, she had to undress in the dark. Her chilled fingers struggled with the waterlogged fabric and fastenings as she listened in dread for anyone's approach. Once her wet clothing was shed she was so much lighter, though still cold. She wrapped herself in a blanket and waited through the night until dawn broke, when she judged it safe to strike a light and dress herself. She could still hear the cries from the men on the water searching from her, but when she peeped out of her hiding place she saw that she and her co-conspirators had planned well, for there were no searchers near the caves.

"Mrs. Ansley had helped me prepare a set of clothes that wouldn't be recognizable as my own," she said. "And then I crept out of the cave and down the shore, away from Sterne House, until I found a path that led up to the road. I carried my old clothes in a bundle, and later we dressed poor Winifred in them."

"And what did you do with—her?"

Rob looked uncomfortable, and Eleanor felt a twinge of sympathy at the sight. It had been difficult for him to use one of his patients, even a deceased one, in so cold a fashion. She knew that the only reason he had brought himself to do it was because of his feelings for Eleanor.

What those feelings were, exactly, was something she would like to know for certain.

Rob cleared his throat. "All we need say is that we kept her in the water, out of the way, and then let her loose to be discovered when we felt the time was right."

"It must have been nerve-wracking," Cecily exclaimed. "I don't think I could have done it."

Eleanor exchanged a look with Rob. "You may find that you have to," she said, as gently as she could.

But the younger woman shuddered, her face screwed up in an expression of horror. "I couldn't. And after all that, to have to make an entirely new life! But then," she added, brightening, "you had a suitor to protect you. How lucky!"

"Well," said Eleanor, and "Er," said Rob. She hoped he would offer clarification of his role—for her sake even more than for Cecily's—but he did not. Finally, when the silence was growing awkward, she said, "Dr. Grant is my employer and friend. It isn't really possible for me to have a suitor until I am free...and I won't be unless Connor Blake divorces me or dies."

Cecily looked taken aback. "Oh. Yes, I see."

"What's more important," Rob said, "is that Eleanor is able to work with me as a nurse and earn her living. Except for the legal fact of her marriage, she has complete independence now."

No, not quite complete. Could any woman be truly independent when she was in love? Eleanor rose to refill the kettle and to give herself a chance to rearrange her face and take a few breaths, and to step away from Rob, whose closeness complicated everything so dreadfully—and so wonderfully.

"The more urgent matter," she said, forcing herself to concentrate on the younger woman's plight, "is what you will do, Cecily. From what I have observed, your position is not as secure as it once was."

"Observed?" she repeated, and then her eyes widened until they seemed about to swallow her face. "You really have been haunting Sterne House? But how? I was nearly convinced we had a ghost!"

Eleanor permitted herself a smile. "You may have noticed that many of the rooms have space behind the walls where they have been altered and modernized. I had become fairly familiar with these areas during my time as mistress of the house, and I made use of them to observe you."

"But why? Were you angry at me for taking your place?"

The kettle came to a boil, and Rob signaled for Eleanor to remain seated while he tended to the tea.

144 | Amanda DeWees

"Not angry—of course not," Eleanor said. "Rather, I was worried. When I saw the announcement of your marriage in the newspaper I knew I needed to find out if you were in danger. So that is why I spied on you—well, initially."

"And did you come to believe I was in danger?" Cecily accepted a mug of tea from Rob without seeming to be aware of it, so urgently were her wide blue eyes fixed upon Eleanor.

"Not at first," Eleanor replied. Rob passed her a cup of tea as well, and she tasted it to find that he had already sweetened it for her. He was thoughtful about things like that. "For a time I thought all was well and that you and he would live happily together."

She didn't speak of the strange pang that had caused her. Not envy exactly, but a bitter feeling that she had failed, that if she had been more like Cecily her husband would never have grown to resent and despise her. It was surprising how much it hurt to find that she had been successfully replaced, even when it was a place she had violently desired to be freed from.

Even though her initial plan had been only to gauge the new bride's safety, she soon realized that she was hoping to learn something else: whether she could have done anything to prevent her marriage from going so wrong. Perhaps she would see something in the way Cecily and Connor behaved with each other that could tell her whether the fault, ultimately, had been her own.

Instead, she saw her husband more clearly. His desire to control his wife through any means at hand, including manipulation and ruthlessness. His ambitions, which took precedence over anyone else's welfare. It had been disturbing to witness the pattern unfolding again, but at least it absolved her of her guilt.

She had felt no sense of triumph, though, while watching and listening to her husband from behind the flimsy paneling, wrapping her arms around herself to try to stop her shaking. Later, when she had gathered her wits sufficiently, she spoke to Mrs. Ansley about arranging a way to meet Cecily and arm her with the truth—distressing though it would be to reveal. She had not expected her to show up quite so soon, though, and so Cecily had caught her off guard.

Perhaps sensing the troubled direction of her thoughts, Rob took up the tale. "As relieved as Eleanor was by her early observations, she had told me that Blake's change of heart toward her had come on some months into the marriage, and for your sake she didn't feel she could afford to assume all would continue as it had begun. So I took this office here, a short journey from Sterne House, where she could come and go with less difficulty."

He said nothing of the upheaval it caused him to relocate. She still marveled at his kindness in doing so much for her sake. Of course, it was also for the welfare of the innocent new wife (or victim) of Connor Blake, but Eleanor suspected that if anyone else had asked it of him he would have refused. She owed him so much that it sometimes overwhelmed her—and yet he had never once so much as hinted that she was in his debt. How extraordinarily fortunate she was to know such a man.

Another man, for example, might have bargained for some benefit to himself for helping her to escape—might have offered his help only in exchange for her becoming his mistress. Never by word or look had Rob suggested such a thing...though Eleanor had to wonder if she would have quashed such a suggestion as quickly as was proper, had it arisen.

Cecily was speaking again. Eleanor reflected with some amusement that speech, not silence, seemed to be the younger woman's preferred state. Then she chided herself. It was equally likely that, isolated as she was, Cecily was merely starved for conversation.

"So you were actually creeping about in the walls to watch us! That is almost as strange a feeling as believing we were haunted. Why did you frighten me by moving the hairbrush?"

It took a moment for Eleanor to realize what she meant. Then she gave a shamefaced laugh. "I was showing off, I'm afraid. It was childish of me."

"I think I can understand," Cecily said, unruffled. "Despite everything, it must have been rather thrilling to play ghost, at least at first. How did you enter the house unseen?"

"The housekeeper is a friend. Without her help it might not have been possible."

Cecily's face reflected her racing thoughts as she no doubt reassessed her knowledge of Mrs. Ansley. "I *thought* she was acting very strangely!" she exclaimed. "First so close-mouthed, then suddenly so helpful. Now I understand why. All the same, weren't you frightened of being discovered? Especially when the builders began work inside?"

"That is why I began to sabotage their work," Eleanor said. "I definitely did not want them to stumble upon me or block up any of my means of entrance and exit, so I hid their tools, damaged their work—whatever I thought might delay or discourage them."

The young woman shook her head in wonder. "It is extraordinary to realize how close you were on so many occasions. How I longed to know more about you, without ever knowing you were practically at my side! If circumstances had been different, we might have been great friends." Then she laughed. "But of course, that would require that we not be married to the same man."

She had nerve, Eleanor had to admit: many another young woman in her position would have fallen to pieces upon learning that she was in a bigamous marriage with a would-be murderer. Not that either had spelled it out in so many words. Perhaps the truth had not fully penetrated yet.

Eleanor said carefully, "I know this must be a great shock to you. To learn that your marriage is not legitimate must be horrifying. But we shall help you in any way that we can. You need not fear that you will be left to fend for yourself as neither a real wife nor a widow."

To her surprise, the young woman began to giggle. Even Rob raised a quizzical eyebrow, and Cecily finally explained, "I was thinking of Freddie, the young man I thought I would marry, and how strongly his parents were opposed to the match simply because I was poor and obscure." The giggle broke out again. "Imagine if they could see me now! How much more scandalous I have become, and through no intention of my own. Why, I am a fallen woman!"

Eleanor and Rob exchanged a look. High spirits were preferable to despair, but in truth the young woman's situation was not something to be taken lightly. Fortunately she was not without resources.

"We can help you craft a new identity, even as we did for Eleanor," Rob said, his voice as kindly and reassuring as when he addressed frail patients on their sickbeds. "It may mean traveling to somewhere that you aren't known, but it can be done."

Cecily found her handkerchief and touched it to the corners of her eyes. Laughter enhanced her beauty, and her eyes were practically sparkling. An anxious twinge took

Eleanor by surprise. It was no wonder Connor had preferred Cecily in her youth and beauty. Might not Rob begin to feel the same way? Both as a doctor and as a man, he could hardly be insensible to the appeal of a pretty young woman in peril.

Eleanor herself had no claims upon him, of course. But she knew now that she wanted to. They must find a time to talk. As delicate as the subject was, she needed to know whether he saw their lives as being intertwined. For if not, she would have to find a way to move forward without him, and that prospect would become more agonizing the longer she worked at his side.

Now, though, was not the time for such reflections. Cecily's life was probably at stake, and that took precedence over any personal matters of the heart. She forced herself to concentrate on what the young woman was saying.

"I suppose I cannot expose him," Cecily mused. "Though it would free me from this pretended marriage, and I would no longer be an obstacle to Connor, it would put you directly at risk again, Eleanor. We mustn't let him know that you are still alive, whatever we do."

The doctor nodded. "The courts could force Eleanor back into residence with him," he said. "She would be at his mercy once again."

"That is a terrifying possibility," Eleanor admitted. The prospect of having to return to Connor Blake frightened her more than she could express—especially because he would undoubtedly resume trying to rid himself of her. "I wish I thought it was possible for me to obtain a divorce, but there is no solid proof of cruelty on his part—and I don't want to involve you, Cecily, as I would have to in order to demonstrate adultery. And then there is the expense."

"We could find the money somehow, or borrow it," Rob said, but she shook her head. Even if they managed to scrape the sum together, it would be a long, grueling, and almost certainly doomed enterprise.

To Cecily she said, "Now that you know everything, do you want to leave him?"

"Leave him!" She was taken aback, but then said slowly, "I suppose that is what I must do. I don't feel safe. But it seems so drastic. Is there no other way?"

Rob leaned his chair back, one foot on the fireplace fender, in his preferred position for thought. "If you think you can change his mind, of course, we can't stop you," he said. "But knowing how violent he has been before, and how ruthless, I think you would be putting yourself in a very dangerous position." Eleanor felt a rush of gratitude for him for taking Cecily's situation so seriously. He continued, "If he did turn against you, you might not have enough time to escape."

"We could make a plan of escape," Cecily suggested, "as the two of you did."

"Our plan was a dangerous one and put Eleanor at great risk." Rob shook his head at the memory. "I don't know if my nerves will ever recover from all the days and nights I worried that Blake would do something terrible before she could escape him. If I were a drinking man, I would have emptied a whole wine cellar."

"You never told me that," Eleanor said.

Ducking his head so that a lock of his brown hair fell in his eyes, he gave his cup of tea a rueful chuckle. "I never intended to," he said. "It doesn't reflect very well on my courage."

Without thinking, she reached out to touch his arm. For an instant he covered her hand with his. Then, when Cecily spoke, he drew it back, and Eleanor did the same.

"You're right," the younger woman said. "It is terribly risky, especially when I know he has a new girl already selected. And if he isn't free to propose to her soon, I fear he may take even more drastic measures."

"A new girl?" Eleanor echoed, and Cecily nodded, her pretty mouth set in a grim line.

"She is from a titled family and walks as if she were wearing ermine and a crown. It was clear at once that Connor is no longer satisfied with the riches he gained from you and now wants aristocratic connections as well. If I had given him a child he might not be so besotted with the idea, but as things stand, I am no longer enough for him."

"Could you lie to him?" Rob suggested. "You could say that you are expecting. It might buy you some time."

"And you could use that as an excuse to escape him," Eleanor added. "Say that the doctor ordered you to spend the rest of your confinement in a hospital because of some complication."

"It might work," Cecily said slowly. "But I shall have to go back in order to persuade him."

"I could write a letter," Rob began, but she shook her head.

"He would not rest until he found me. Even if he no longer wants me, he wouldn't want me to leave of my own volition, doctor or no. Especially if that doctor was you, Dr. Grant."

"He loathes me," Rob acknowledged. "We would need another doctor, and another person in on the secret means that much more chance of our plan being exposed."

"And that would mean time too," Eleanor said. "We couldn't hope to induce anyone to join us without making our case in person, which requires traveling." She looked helplessly at the doctor. "Cecily may indeed have to return. Even if it is only for a day or two."

"Could you return as well, Eleanor?" she begged. "I should feel much safer if I knew you were close by."

"I don't think that would be safe," Rob said before she could form an answer. "It is Eleanor's decision, of course, but I vote against it."

"What if we were both to confront him at once," the fair-haired young woman said, "and before plenty of witnesses? Then he would be unable to harm us."

"What do you have in mind?" Eleanor asked.

"Connor's newest caprice is a masked ball to celebrate the completion of the underwater ballroom."

"The what?" Eleanor interrupted before she could speak further. "What are you talking about?"

Cecily gave her a martyred look that reminded Eleanor of how very young she was. "One of his whims is to make Sterne House into a great showplace," she sighed. "He is having a huge domed ballroom constructed at the bottom of the artificial lake, with passages leading from the house. It sounds as though it will be quite spectacular, I admit. And in order to impress our visitors, he has announced that there will be an extravagant party to christen the room."

"A masked ball," Rob said thoughtfully. "There are possibilities there. It might well be the safest means for Eleanor and me to insinuate ourselves into the house."

"And plenty of witnesses if we chose to confront him," Eleanor added.

Cecily sat up straight, as alert as a beagle who scented a trail. "Would you accuse him then? Let everyone know how he had attempted to kill you? If he is startled and frightened by your suddenly seeming to come back from the dead, he might say something incriminating that you could use to obtain a divorce."

Hope struggled with caution in Eleanor's mind. Such an admission in itself might not be sufficient. Eleanor knew a bit more than Cecily seemed to about the process of obtaining a divorce, enough to know that as a woman she was highly unlikely to be granted one despite the circumstances. But if Connor himself were to initiate the proceedings...perhaps after all there might be a way for her to slip the shackles of her marriage.

"If he admitted before witnesses that he tried to kill me," she mused, "that would give me a certain amount of power over him. Perhaps in exchange for my not going to the authorities he would agree to seek a divorce himself. He would be much more likely to succeed than I." Then she hesitated, looking at Rob. "But he would have to claim adultery," she said slowly, "and even though we know it isn't true, it could still destroy your good name, Rob."

Rob said firmly, "If I must fall upon that sword, I'll not hesitate to do so."

Eleanor looked at him in wonder. That was no small gesture, for his medical practice would suffer if he became involved in a marital scandal. The knowledge that he would sacrifice his reputation on her behalf made her heart constrict painfully with gratitude and love.

All unaware of her thoughts, Rob continued, "But there will be time to worry about such details later, and it looks as though our being at the ball offers the best means of freeing the both of you. When is this extravaganza to be?"

"In March, or at least that is his present intention," Cecily told them. "If I send you word through Mrs. Ansley, can we remain in contact?"

"As long as you are very careful what you put in writing," Eleanor said. "Let's invent a doctor with whom you can correspond so that Connor won't suspect anything should he see the address."

"What fun!" Cecily exclaimed. "I shall feel delightfully like a spy sending messages from behind enemy lines."

It was on the tip of Eleanor's tongue to warn her against such excitement, to remind her how grave her situation was. But she kept silent. The girl was young, but no fool; she was not insensible to her peril, and if she found any part of it enjoyable, that was probably better for her state of mind—and it might prevent Connor from recognizing how much she knew.

Rob suggested, "Perhaps if you start each letter with a lengthy description of symptoms of impending motherhood, the more explicit the better, anyone who might be surreptitiously reading will give up and cease to pay attention. It could make it easier to hide any news of importance. Do you need any information in that line?"

Cecily shook her bright head, making her earrings dance. "Believe me, I have heard plenty of old ladies talk about all the disgusting things that happen to a woman who is expecting. I shan't run out of revolting symptoms to describe!" She bounced up from her chair, caught up her fur-trimmed mantle, and held out her hand to Eleanor. "I must be going now, or he will begin to miss me. I feel as though I've discovered a sister. This may sound peculiar, but please believe I am wholly sincere when I say how glad I am that you aren't dead!"

It felt good to laugh at her situation for a change. Impulsively, Eleanor reached out to embrace the younger woman. "In that we are of one mind," she said. "Will you be safe, though, Cecily?"

The young woman's nod was certain. "I am on my guard now, and at my first opportunity I shall tell Connor I am in an interesting condition. If he is not overjoyed...well, I shall simply find a way to escape and come back to you!"

CHAPTER ELEVEN
Cecily

O n the drive back to Sterne House, Cecily's mind was abuzz with all of the surprises of the morning. Eleanor Blake alive! She marveled at the courage and cleverness it had taken to effect her escape. And how lovely to find that she was so nice—watching over her all this time, more like a guardian angel than a ghost, had she but realized.

All the same, despite her avowed confidence, she was not certain returning to Sterne House was as safe as she had declared. The trouble was that she had no faith that staying away would be any safer. Connor could be frightening in his singlemindedness, and she knew that if she went away he would stop at nothing to get her back—even if it was only so that he could kill her.

If only she could tell him that she was not his legal wife and was thus no impediment to him! But if Connor learned that Eleanor was still alive, that would mean nothing but danger for her.

Cecily decided she might as well begin her masquerade as an expectant mother at once and spent the return journey humming to herself with what she hoped was a dreamy expression in case the coachman should observe her. But when he left her, as she requested, at the back garden near the kitchen entrance, her humming dwindled and stopped.

The bleak expanse of Sterne House rising before her had a chilling effect on her excitement. Its grim, uncompromising facade might as well have been that of a prison. How foolish she had been to think it would be easy to escape this fortress and its owner. She felt small and powerless here in the shadow of the towers, as if all of her plans were doomed to futility.

She was startled out of these depressing thoughts when a voice came out of nowhere. In a hissing whisper, it said, "Cecily! I have found you!"

Whirling, she found herself still alone. The high hedges were shivering as if under a strong wind, but there was no wind.

Staring hard, she approached the section whose leaves were most agitated. "Who is there?" she whispered.

More shaking of leaves, and then a face emerged. An impossibly familiar face, with ingenuous blue eyes and surmounted by tousled blond hair. "Freddie?" she squeaked.

"Hush! No one must know I am here." Freddie Hightower scanned the yard behind Cecily. He was so incongruous in these surroundings that he might have been a visitant from another world.

How little changed he was, when she felt she had become almost another person in the time since they parted. His fair hair was still cut in the same style; his clothing, though in muted colors presumably selected to be inobtrusive, was still the very height of fashion. With his striped waistcoat and twilled silk tie he might have just come from exercising his horse in Rotten Row.

"I have stumbled upon a secret about your husband," he said urgently. "You must know the truth."

She suspected he was rather enjoying the drama of his daring feat. And while she was flattered by the lengths to which he had gone to protect her interests, his presence was most inconvenient to say the least. "It's shockingly dangerous for you to be here," she said.

"Not for me," he said boastfully. "I carry a pistol everywhere I go now. If your husband tries anything, I shall be ready!"

She suppressed a groan. He sounded as though he had been reading American dime novels about desperadoes in the Wild West. As perhaps he had.

"Even if you aren't worried about your own skin, you might think of mine," she said. "If Connor finds you here he will think it's because I asked you to come. You must go at once."

"Not without warning you." Again he looked around to make certain they were alone. A branch poked him in the nose, and he swatted at it irritably, causing leaves to detach from a branch and float gently to the ground. Unobtrusive he was not.

But he might have learned something useful. "Warning me of what?"

He whispered, "The man you are married to is not Connor Blake."

"What!" She wasn't certain whether to believe him or not. "Then who is he?"

"I don't know his real name yet. But the real Connor Blake was a war hero who died at Inkerman. I was talking to a chap at my club, and it came out that he knew the real Blake and saw him cut down in battle. He showed me a photograph of the two of them, and although there was a passing resemblance, the man in the picture was definitely not the man you married." When she did not reply at once, he reached for her hand. "You've married an impostor, Cecily. He could be anybody—a bigamist, even a convict! And it's all my fault. We must find a way to extricate you from this terrible mess."

Her mind was too busy with her own thoughts to pay full attention to his distress. Did Eleanor know of her husband's assumed identity? Almost certainly not, or she would have mentioned it. So Connor—or the man bearing that name—had courted and married Eleanor under false pretenses. Had he served at all in the war?

As dangerous as she already knew him to be, it was still shocking to learn there were even more layers to his deceit and ruthlessness. Cecily felt as though she could not be certain of anything about him now. A wave of cold flooded her veins.

"You must go," she whispered. "Thank you for telling me this, but you mustn't stay."

He made no move to extricate himself from his hiding place. "We must get you away from here. Only then can I confront him."

"Confront him!" Alarm made the words emerge loudly, and she lowered her voice once more. "That would be foolhardy, Freddie. Men have killed to keep lesser secrets than this."

"I shall bring the authorities, then. My friend and I can go to the police with his photograph and—"

The creak of a door made him fall silent. The footman William was emerging from the house and approaching down the path. Cecily moved closer to the hedge in an attempt to shield its occupant from sight.

"Begging your pardon, madam," the footman said, "but the master requests that you join him in his study."

"Very well. Can you tell him I shall be a few minutes more?"

But the man drew ever nearer. "He wishes for you to join him right away, madam. He asked me to escort you in."

If only she could have had a few more minutes alone with Freddie! But if Connor was already in an ill humor, she ought to set about pacifying him without delay. She reluctantly made her way up the path toward William.

"After luncheon perhaps I shall be able to take a turn about the garden," she said, hoping that Freddie would hear and understand that he should remain there. But then she remembered that she was supposed to be in an Interesting Condition—and that Connor was likely to be the protective type of husband who would want to circumscribe her movements.

With an effort, she refrained from glancing back at Freddie's hiding place. Perhaps she could send the housekeeper out to find him and either send him on his way or—if he proved stubborn—help him to find a better place of concealment, before he got both himself and Cecily into trouble.

Fortunately, Connor was every bit as thrilled by her news as she had hoped he would be—and just as easily fooled.

"A baby?" he said, his voice tender and wondering. "Is it really true?"

"It is," she lied, beaming at him in relief, and he caught her up in his arms to hold her tightly before coming to himself.

"But I must remember to treat you gently," he said. His dark eyes were soft with happiness, and at this moment she could almost forget how dangerous—how frightening—he could be. She even felt a twinge of doubt, almost like guilt, when he asked, "Shouldn't you be in bed?"

"That is still a fair way off. The doctor said—"

"What sort of doctor is he?"

"The village doctor. His name is, ah, Roberts. He is most agreeable."

Some of the delight ebbed from his eyes. "Young, is he?"
"Oh, no, I wouldn't say so. He has a beard and everything. At any rate, he believes I am as healthy as a horse, provided I take the usual precautions."

Still he was not in an entirely good humor. "What put it into your head to go gadding about in the village instead of sending for the doctor to come here?"

She allowed an injured look to come into her face. "Why, when I slipped and fell into the pit it scared me half to death. I already suspected that I might be in the family way, and I was terrified that the fall might have hurt the baby. I was too frightened to sit about waiting. And aren't you glad I didn't? Now I can share my news with you without any worries!"

More gently than before, Connor took her in his arms and pressed his lips to her forehead. "My darling girl, how happy you have made me. I can't wait to announce the news."

"Announce it! My goodness, no, you ridiculous man! How embarrassed I should be!" But she was delighted with the idea. She had clearly secured his good graces again.

When Connor shared the news with their guests, the Longhurst family congratulated them but decided to cut their visit short, judging that they were in the way. Cecily was relieved. Having Augusta there seemed to tantalize Connor, and Cecily would feel immeasurably safer with them gone.

While they were making preparations to leave and the servants were packing their trunks, Cecily contrived to confer with Mrs. Ansley in her little parlor in the servants' quarters. When she revealed that she had met Eleanor, a brief play of emotions was visible in Mrs. Ansley's face before she was able to control her reaction.

"I hope, madam, that you were able to look past your differences to your common cause," she said.

"Yes, never fear. I liked her enormously, and I believe she had every right to do as she did."

"And Mr. Blake—?"

"I shall tell him nothing, not until she is ready to reveal herself to him." Seeing that the older woman still looked anxious, she added, "I have no wish to make my false marriage into a real one. Eleanor is no obstacle to me." It would be difficult going back to her old life of parasitic penury, to be sure, but that was a thousand times better than being yoked to a man who wished her dead.

Relief made the housekeeper look more animated than Cecily had yet seen her. "I am so relieved to hear you say that, madam," she exclaimed. "With us working together, we can see justice done."

Cecily eyed her with interest. "Mrs. Ansley, as grateful as I am for your assistance, I am curious: I should think it would be safer for you to side with the master of the house in all things. Why do you risk your position and his fury by working to further Eleanor's and my interests?"

The housekeeper's expression turned remote, and for some moments Cecily thought she would refuse to answer. But she did, albeit in a voice so low that Cecily had to strain to hear her.

"I was married myself, once. It was a long time ago, when I was too young to understand that charm and a handsome face were not signs of character."

"What happened?"

Quietly Mrs. Ansley said, "He had a vicious temper. I lost a pregnancy because of him. Now I realize that that might have been a more merciful fate than being born only to fall victim to his violence."

On impulse, Cecily reached out to squeeze the other woman's arm, but the housekeeper stepped away from the touch, and Cecily realized that she must not force closeness between them if the other woman did not wish it. "I am so sorry," she said, hoping to convey in her tone what she had not been able to by touch. "That sounds horrific."

The housekeeper's nod was very slight. Perhaps she had to work to maintain her composure when discussing such sensitive things and feared that her emotions would overflow if she did not keep a tight rein on them. And little wonder, with so much pain in her past.

"He died," she said, almost distantly. "Stupidly, in some pub brawl. I wanted to sing when I learned of it. But I didn't, of course." A quick, wry smile flashed briefly and was gone. "His mother still believes he was a paragon among men, and she is a good woman, so I have not had the heart to disillusion her."

Cecily doubted she herself could have been so magnanimous. "And naturally your experiences made you sympathetic to Eleanor."

"When I saw what she was enduring, when I realized that her life was at risk, I had to help her. Just as I will help you."

A peremptory knock forestalled Cecily's reply, and William the footman called through the door that the guests were ready to depart and Mr. Blake wished for Cecily to join him in seeing them off.

"It seems I must go," Cecily said. There was so much still to discuss with her new ally, and to learn about her. Perhaps her supposed pregnancy would make her husband less demanding of her presence. "Oh! I should tell you, I am pretending to be with child," she whispered, mindful of the footman on the other side of the door. "Because of Mr.

Blake, you understand. I should so much appreciate your help with that pretense."

"Of course," Mrs. Ansley said, likewise in a whisper. "I think that is a sound idea."

"There is one more thing. A young man is concealing himself in the garden. I should be grateful if you could induce him to go. He means well, but his presence is most inconvenient."

"Very well," said Mrs. Ansley, and Cecily marveled again at her calmness. Then the housekeeper opened the door. "Mrs. Blake just wished to discuss the menu with me," she told the footman. "Some changes were recommended by her doctor. You may accompany her to her husband now."

Her slender, black-clad form receded from view as Cecily hurried down the corridor with her escort. Whoever would have guessed that the prim, reticent mistress of the servants had endured so much—and was capable of so much?

To Cecily's great relief, her announcement seemed to have won Connor back. His dark moods disappeared, and he was as affectionate as he had been during the first weeks of their marriage. And how easy her deception was! Her husband, like so many men of his class, had been shut out of the childbearing process in the name of decency, so he knew only what he had been able to glean. It was enough for her to show revulsion at certain foods, pretend to be ill from time to time, and display a more than usual tendency for taking naps.

But Freddie remained, and that was a problem.

She had expected that, once Mrs. Ansley had discouraged him, he would give up on this foolhardy errand and return to the world where he belonged. As days elapsed, though, she began to realize she had done him an injustice. Freddie actually had changed. Despite all common sense or risk to himself, he had taken a room in the village and had even contrived to send her word of this by way of Mrs. Ansley, "in case you should need me," he wrote. He even had the good sense to leave the note unsigned and worded in such a way that if anyone else had intercepted it they might have believed it to be a love note for one of the maids. In all ways he was minimizing the risk to her. But Cecily knew that if Connor somehow learned that her onetime beau was in the vicinity, he would at once seize upon the worst possible explanation for his presence. And Connor's jealousy, once awakened, might be terrifying. The best thing for her, and for Freddie, would be for him to leave Cecily behind. After all, he had done so once before.

But perhaps for that very reason, he refused to do the sensible thing now. For good or ill, Freddie had now become the most stubbornly loyal of suitors—long after she truly needed him to be.

CHAPTER TWELVE
Eleanor

Eleanor had hoped that after relating their story to Cecily she and Rob would continue to talk, discussing the things that had never been said between them about their feelings and their future. But then came a summons from a patient who had broken her leg, and Rob and Eleanor went to attend to her without having said a word to each other on any subject more personal than bone fractures.

Sometimes Eleanor thought that she and Rob were growing closer. Tonight, for example, when she was elbow deep in plaster of Paris creating a cast for the patient, a strand of her hair worked its way free of her hairpins and fell into her eyes. Rob went to her and gently secured it again. Was it her imagination, or did he let his hand linger on her hair? But when she looked up and began to thank him, he said crisply, "I can't believe that with all the scientific advances at our disposal no one has managed to invent hairpins that will do their job adequately."

And he was strangely gruff when leaving parting instructions for the patient's husband. Usually Rob was kind and reassuring, but tonight he seemed almost angry when he informed old Mr. Petherbridge that the house needed to be made safer.

"This is Mrs. Petherbridge's second fall in two months," he said. "At her age, the next could well be fatal. For that matter, it would be better for both of you to have all the rugs taken up."

Distress showed in the elderly man's faded eyes as he glanced at the closed door behind which his wife lay with her leg in the fresh plaster cast. "But Sarah loves them so. She takes so much pride in the house. To tell her the rugs must be removed would distress her terribly." He lowered his voice even further. "I couldn't bear to make her cry, doctor."

Eleanor saw Rob's chest swell as he took a deep breath, but it must have been an effort to calm himself, for his voice was still pitched low when he replied, "Nevertheless it must be done. If she cries, so be it—her tears will end, and life will go on. Whereas if you try to spare her feelings by leaving all of these hazards lying about, you practically guarantee she will fall again. Next time she might strike her head, or she could contract pneumonia while she convalesces. Falls are quite serious in people of her years."

"But, doctor—"

"The choice is simple," Rob snapped. "You may have a sad wife or a dead one."

Eleanor felt a pang of sympathy for old Mr. Petherbridge, who looked shaken by this ruthless dictum. But Rob was right, though he was usually more tactful.

When they left, afternoon was turning to dusk, and the setting sun revealed weary lines around Rob's eyes. And probably her own, though she had no mirror in which to check. He glanced at her as they set out down the street.

"Was I too harsh with him, do you think?"

"You spoke with authority."

He sighed. "I suppose I was too severe. It's just absurd to me that someone would rather put his wife's life in danger than risk making her unhappy for a few hours or days." He ruminated on this a few minutes more, then brightened at the sight of a tea stall.

"Let's stop and get some tea," he said. "I'm worn out, and you must be as well."

The hot tea seemed to improve his disposition, and some of the strain left his face. Eleanor, watching him through the vapor rising from her own cup, reflected on how rarely she had seen him lose his temper. Which was curious, since he had been so out of temper on the occasion when they first met. She recalled how he had apologized, explaining that his strong feelings about the hospital had made him fly off the handle. And tonight, she suspected, it was because he was so worried about his patient that he had become uncharacteristically snappish.

But even before that he had been short with her about her hair, although his fingers had been gentle when he had tucked it back into the hairpins. And he had been startlingly gruff with her sometimes before—often just when they had seemed to be getting along well.

"You're very quiet," he observed at length. "Tired out, are you?"

"A bit." And turning things over in her mind in the light of a new perspective.

"We'll strike out for home, then. You've worked hard."

"So have you," she said.

By the time they returned to Rob's office night had fallen, and the landlady had left a lamp burning in the office. They did not light another, since they needed little illumination to wash their hands, the first order of business after so messy a house call.

The china basin was just large enough that they could both wash up at once, and they had done it dozens of times; it was one of the little incidental intimacies they had gradually fallen into that Eleanor told herself meant nothing. But this evening, the second or third time their hands bumped against each other, Rob took one of her hands in his, palm up, and lifted it out of the water.

"Your hands have changed so much," he mused. "They used to be immaculate." He stroked his thumb over a long scratch, then touched a fading bruise, and she caught her breath. "Now they have battle scars."

"But now they're useful," she said. "That's what gives my life meaning, being useful—"

"To our patients."

"And to you." Slowly, so as not to startle him, she turned her hand over and clasped his. For a moment he was motionless. Then, to her delight, his strong, blunt fingers closed around hers.

Still staring at her hand in his, he said in a low voice, "I've tried to be mindful of your delicate situation. The last thing I want is to take advantage of your position in any way, or make you feel that you owe me anything just because I helped you."

"You never have."

"It would be different if you were free to marry. But as things are..."

As things were, she realized she had seen him catch himself many times when they were feeling any fashion of intimacy with each other. One minute they would be laughing together, and the next he would go suddenly brusque and change the topic to something innocuous and proper.

It wasn't coincidence. He cared.

"As things are," he repeated, "it's crucial that you know you can trust in my respect for you."

"I do." Then, daring greatly, "And I trust your love for me, all the more because you've never breathed a word of it."

He looked suddenly younger in his bewilderment. "How did you know?"

"I didn't, until now." She could not keep from smiling, and he laughed self-consciously.

"I walked right into that," he said. "And here I prided myself on how magnificently I was concealing how I felt."

"Well, I'm hardly an impartial observer. I just started to realize that you are at your grumpiest when things between us seem to be going well. It made me suspect—and if this is vanity on my part, I will be justly rebuked—it made me suspect that you were out of sorts because you wanted us to be together but thought we couldn't."

He said carefully, "I don't want to make any assumptions."

"All you need do is ask, Rob."

In the lamplight, his usually frank blue eyes were shadowed. "I was too frightened that you would go."

Joy was beginning to quicken her breath. "Do you really feel so strongly about us? Because even though Eleanor Blake cannot marry you, Nurse Jones can."

"You would be content with a sham marriage?" he exclaimed. "You deserve better, Eleanor."

"It isn't a sham if we make it real for ourselves. I know you're a man of honor, and I believe you would respect me as much as you would a legal wife."

He raised his other hand, although it was dripping with water, to touch her face. "I want to be sure I understand. If you are willing to marry me..."

She covered his hand with hers. "I mean that I love you, Rob. I do." Giddy in her happiness, she raised her face to his and kissed him. After a moment of paralysis he kissed her back, gently at first as though afraid of frightening her away, then exuberantly, and his arms slipped around her waist to hold her tight. Her body felt brimming over with joy, as if it could not contain so much happiness and love. When at last they parted, they could not help laughing breathlessly at each other. His eyes were warm, the smiling crinkles at the corners of his eyes pronounced in the lamplight, and he gazed at her with a wondering look.

Resting his forehead against hers, he murmured, "What do we do now?"

She did not think he meant it as a leading question. Perhaps he was feeling overwhelmed...as was she, though in the most beautiful way.

"We've had a dreadfully long day, and I imagine we're both exhausted," she said. "Perhaps we should sleep on all of this." This joy was so new she was almost afraid to trust it yet.

He rubbed his cheek against hers, and the unexpected silkiness of his beard against her skin sent a delicious shiver through her. "A night's sleep won't change my mind," he said softly into her ear. "Or my heart."

"Nor mine," she promised.

"Until the morning, then." He kissed her again, with a tenderness that melted her very bones, and she began to wonder if it was insanity to think of spending the rest of the night apart. Then he drew back, gazing at her.

"I'm not usually so tentative," he said. "I'm much more accustomed to forging ahead when something is important to me—you may have observed that."

She smiled. "There is much to be said for forging ahead."

"But you mean the world to me, Eleanor, and I don't want to risk wrecking what we've found by thoughtlessly blundering forward." Taking a deep breath, he released her and stepped back. "So I'll say good night."

Slightly disappointed despite herself, she echoed, "Good night."

It seemed he was not going to move until she left, so she lit a candle and made for the stairs. At the threshold she turned to look back, and he was still standing watching her, his hands in his pockets and a dazed happiness on his face.

That was how she left him. Up in her chilly room she set about undressing, laughing to herself every now and then in sheer exhilaration. After she climbed into bed, shivering, she lay thinking about him, replaying all that he had said, picturing him, recalling the softness of his lips on hers. Everything was different now, after just a few words exchanged. Her life had been transformed.

Her thoughts were so full of wonder, and of him, that she could not sleep. After a while she lit the candle again and looked at the time.

Nearly half an hour had passed since they had parted. Would he be asleep? Sheer physical exhaustion might have claimed him.

Suddenly she could not bear the thought of being away from him. Even if it were only to steal a glimpse of his face, she wanted to be with him again. Rising, she put on her dressing gown and took up the candle.

Though she knew the landlady to be hard of hearing, she made her way cautiously, avoiding the floorboards that were known to creak. The door to Rob's bedchamber was closed. She thought of knocking, then thought better of it. Thought of trying the handle, then thought better of that as well.

Suddenly the door opened, and she and Rob both started at the shock of seeing the other. His hair was rumpled, and he had evidently begun to undress, as his shirt was half unbuttoned. She saw a scattering of silky dark hairs on the area of his chest thus revealed. It was the most intimate glimpse she had yet had of his body, and it stirred something within her.

He looked almost abashed when he said, "I decided I couldn't wait until morning to see you again."

She said, "I decided the same thing. May I come in?"

His eyes brightened, and his lips curved in a smile that had a touch of mischief. "You certainly may," he said.

She stepped into the room. He shut the door firmly behind her, and they were not parted again that night.

CHAPTER THIRTEEN
Cecily

ecily had assured her husband that she would still be able to attend social functions by the time the masked ball came about, and in his delight at incipient fatherhood he wanted to show her off, so there was no objection to her attending the ball. After deliberation, he decided her costume should represent a water spirit. Cecily told him that Mrs. Ansley was helping her with it, so that there would be an innocent reason for them to shut themselves up together.

The costume itself was designed to show off Connor's wealth—or, rather, Eleanor's. Cecily was all too aware now that every single morsel of food and scrap of clothing in Sterne House was paid for with Eleanor's money and was being stolen from her in a sense. But of course she could say nothing of that, and she knew that Connor wanted her to present herself as the embodiment of his supposed worth, so when he told her to spare no expense she did as bidden.

Sewn in varying shades of green, her costume had an ethereal overskirt of sea green tulle covered with brilliant spangles and medieval-style pointed sleeves that reached the ground. Brilliant insect wings were painstakingly embroidered over the bodice in a pattern mimicking fish scales, and she was to wear a silvery coronet fashioned with shells.

Connor himself would be Neptune, in a Renaissance-style doublet of silver brocade and a long cape of shot silk that iridesced from silver to green. He would have a coronet made in the form of coral branches and a trident set with real pearls. Cecily had not realized before how vain her husband was, but his determination to get every single detail of his costume right revealed just how particular he could be about how he presented himself.

But of course, she realized, he was essentially displaying himself as an attractive matrimonial prospect to Augusta Norris and perhaps other unattached young women at the ball. If he made a strong impression now with this display of wealth and taste, his eventual courtship would go that much more smoothly once he was a wealthy widower and Cecily was out of the way. It was gruesome to see him laying the groundwork for his life after her death.

He took to staying up late mulling over plans for the house and the ball, so she went to bed alone as often as not. He had a bed made up in his dressing room so he would not disturb her when he retired late. It was rather a relief, all things considered, for she was nervous that in close quarters he would notice that her body had not changed at all as a result of this supposed pregnancy.

But one night he burst into their bedroom after she had fallen asleep. She woke to a dark figure shaking her by the shoulders and growling questions at her.

"What?" she said in confusion. "What is it?"

"Where is that paper you found in my bureau? The ledger page? I know you have it."

Sleep-dazed as she was, it took her a moment to comprehend what he was talking about. When her drowsy brain caught his meaning, she said, "I haven't seen it since that night, Connor. After you scolded me so, I never went looking for it again."

"It is missing." The firelight was behind him, so she could not see his face. His dark silhouette looming over her was menacing, and the tone of his voice was a warning.

"Perhaps you locked it in the safe and just forgot," she suggested.

"It isn't in the safe, devil take it!"

She could hear the frustration in his voice and tried to placate him. "I truly don't have it, Connor. Might one of the servants have found it? Perhaps one of the maids moved it when putting fresh linen in your bureau." Ordinarily she wouldn't have foisted blame onto anyone else, but at this moment her mind was flailing about for any way to save herself.

He moved suddenly, and her heart lurched—but he was moving away from her. She felt her body sag with relief.

"I'm sure you'll find it in the morning," she said. "No doubt after some sleep you'll remember where you put James Snow."

Instantly she knew she had said the wrong thing. He whirled and seized her by the shoulders once more. "What do you know about James Snow?" he demanded.

"Nothing! Nothing at all. I just remembered the name. Please, Connor, you're being a bit rough. The baby, you know..."

For a moment his painful grip on her did not ease. Then, blessedly, he loosened his hands and finally released her. She could hear him breathing.

At last he said, in a quiet voice more frightening than bluster, "You must forget James Snow, Cecily. Forget you ever saw the name."

"Very well."

"Promise."

She drew in a breath, feeling the panicked flutter of her heart. "I promise. I give you my word."

He gave no sign that he had heard her. But after a few moments, he stood and crossed the room. At the threshold he turned and said softly, "Mind your promise, my dear."

"Yes, Connor." Only by the fiercest effort of will did she keep her voice from shaking.

She slept little the rest of the night. Connor did not return, and she supposed that he had retired to his dressing room. She wished she could lock the doors, but she did not dare.

In the days that followed, Connor remained gruff and preoccupied, despite her dropping mentions of the purported baby into the conversation. He did not mention the missing paper again, but from his ill humor she guessed that it had not been found.

One morning he entered her room as she was dressing and came to put his arms around her, one hand going to her stomach. She thought at first he meant it as affection.

"You're very lovesome this morning," she said, smiling at him in the mirror. It would be a relief if his dark mood had eased.

But he didn't return her smile. In the mirror, his face was morose. "You're still quite slender," he said. "Shouldn't the baby be growing?"

"Sometimes it takes a long time for them to show," she said, careful not to let her smile falter. "That's what the doctor said, and Mrs. Ansley says the same. It is different from woman to woman."

"Still...ought we to call in another doctor? I'm not sure anyone from the village knows what he is about. Let me write to someone from London."

And have him recognize her charade within five minutes? "Dearest, that's too much trouble and expense. I'm sure I shall begin to put on weight as soon as I stop being sick in the mornings. Just now it's difficult to keep food down." She stretched up to kiss him, putting every ounce of feminine witchery that she could into her lips, and stroked her hands over his shirt front. "You're such a dear husband to be so concerned for the baby's welfare," she said in a softer voice. "But how are you, my darling? You look as if something is weighing on you."

"It's nothing."

"I will help in any way I can," she said cajolingly, and he softened at last.

"With so many important people coming to the ball, I'm worried that they won't feel adequately feted. Perhaps you can go over the menu and decorations with me and Mrs. Ansley."

"Of course," she exclaimed, relieved that the solution was so easy. "I shall be more than happy to."

"And also discuss accommodations? We've a great many aristocratic families attending, and it would be humiliating if they found their quarters here insufficiently luxurious."

She managed to keep from making a wry rejoinder. In her experience, aristocratic homes were all too likely to be reduced by the passage of years to drafty, empty, under-staffed shells that sapped the family resources while moldering gently to ruin.

"I'm sure Sterne House will do you proud," she said. "But if you would like to go over the guest list with me, I shall be happy to advise you as best I can."

"Excellent. Though you won't be the equal of our guests socially, you do have native good taste." While she was silent with bemusement at this assessment of her, he kissed her on the brow. He really was quite handsome he was when in a good temper. "Come to my study when you are finished dressing, and we will get to work," he said, and left her.

Once Cecily was established at his desk with her husband, however, she found the guest list disquieting. There were so few people that she had met, and the list overwhelmingly favored titled families. Even more troubling was the number of unattached young women there. It seemed that almost every peer or peeress was accompanied by a daughter.

But perhaps she was misreading things. "I declare, what a lot of children will be coming," she said brightly. "It will be such fun to have little ones about the place, especially with ours on the way."

Connor bent over the paper so that she could not see his face. "Our guests will only be bringing their children who are of age," he said. "Youngsters would only be a nuisance at a ball."

"Yes, of course," she said, feeling dread sink into her belly like a weight. "You are quite right."

Enlightenment came from an unexpected source. Two days later when she was listlessly walking in the kitchen garden, shredding a spray of lavender in her hand for the soothing fragrance, a piercing whisper seized her attention.

"Cecily! Over here!"

The voice came from a recess near the kitchen door. It was Freddie, of course, a bit more disheveled than before, but with triumph in his eyes and a piece of paper in his hand. She recognized it at once as the ledger page whose absence had caused her husband to fly into such a rage.

"What are you doing with that?" she hissed. "How did you even get it?"

"I bribed one of the footmen. He may yet betray me, but it will be worth it if this means what I think it does."

Half her mind was still occupied with the troubling prospect of a corruptible footman when he asked in an injured tone, "Don't you want to know what it is?"

"Yes, of course. Tell me." Glancing around to make certain they were unobserved, she drew closer to his hiding place. He was dressed more inconspicuously than before, in a mismatched woolen coat and trousers that showed some wear, rather than his usual tailored elegance. It suited him, to her surprise; he looked more mature.

His grin was conspiratorial. "It's a page from the records of a foundling home," he said.

"What? How do you know?"

"I just had to find the right people to ask. Evidently, when a woman surrenders her baby to one of these places, they cut a scrap of fabric from her dress and keep it with the record of the date and name. That way, if the mother's fortunes ever improve and she wishes to find her child again, they can match the dress with the scrap." He held up the page with its snippet of fabric. "These unfortunates rarely give their true name," Freddie continued, "so this method of identification is the best they can manage."

"So James Snow is probably an alias."

"Almost certainly."

"What on earth is Connor doing with his record?" Then belated understanding made her gasp so loudly she clapped her hand over her mouth. More quietly she said, "Connor is James Snow? He was a foundling?"

Freddie nodded vigorously. His blue eyes were bright with excitement. "I believe so. That means that he may be lying about his past—parts of it, even all of it. Cecily, I am sorry to tell you this, but your husband could be absolutely anyone—or anything."

The words haunted her. Connor, or James, had risen from nothing by dint of stealing the identity of a war hero, then marrying a wealthy woman. In marrying Cecily, had he been following his heart for once instead of his self-interest? She remembered his tenderness toward her in the early weeks of her marriage and thought perhaps it was so. At the same time, though, he had loved to show her off, especially in those early months. He had taken pride in how many invitations they received, how much pleasure other men took in Cecily's youth and attractiveness, enhanced as it was in the gowns and jewels he had lavished upon her. Cecily had been a good calling card in those days, a social advantage, and she gathered that Eleanor had not had such a stimulating effect on Connor's social calendar. Eleanor's money had opened doors for him, but Cecily herself had opened many more.

And now, it seemed, he wanted to raise his status yet again, by marrying into a titled family. That would be a triumph for the onetime foundling child. Whether it would be enough to satisfy him was another question. If he were to dispose of Cecily and marry a peer's daughter, would he later decide that even she was not enough to satisfy his ambition?

All these thoughts ran through her head in moments. When she came to herself, Freddie was gently, urgently repeating her name. His candid blue eyes were worried.

"Ought I not to have told you?" he asked. "You look dreadful."

"No, I am glad you told me. But give the paper back to me now." If she could return it to Connor's room without being seen, perhaps his agitation would be eased somewhat.

And perhaps she might then be able to feel safe again— at least for a little while.

With unusual tact, Freddie did not press her for explanations or details. He handed her the page, which she tucked into her sleeve. She thanked him with a nod. As she opened the kitchen door and stepped into the house, she was aware of his troubled gaze following her.

Well might he be troubled, she thought wryly. She herself was more troubled than he could possibly dream. This clue to her husband's past, and his present intentions, made her feel more imperiled than ever.

What could she do, short of inventing a fictitious titled forebear, to keep herself safe until the ball? Be at her most charming, most solicitous, most...convincingly pregnant?

Or perhaps making herself scarce would be wiser. She thought of the hiding places that Eleanor had told her about, but she needed a better solution—a more permanent one.

The fact of the matter was that, if she could have done so without putting Eleanor in danger, she would have loved nothing more than to flee Sterne House, never to return.

CHAPTER FOURTEEN
Eleanor

"I'm frightened," Eleanor said.

Rob put his hands on her shoulders. He was standing behind her at the mirror where she stood regarding her costume for the Sterne House ball, for which they would be departing soon.

"That's perfectly natural," he said. "You needn't do this if you don't want to, you know. We can move away from here and establish ourselves as a married couple. I doubt Blake would ever find us."

She shook her head, and her paste earrings glinted in the light. She was dressed in the style of Marie Antoinette, with a white wig and a lace-trimmed pink dress. She had chosen the costume primarily for the wig, which made her nearly unrecognizable, and the fact that she knew it would be a popular disguise. She wanted to be as inconspicuous as possible right up until she decided to confront Connor. Cecily had managed to smuggle invitations to her and Rob under assumed names, and it would be best if no one looked at them too closely or questioned the unfamiliar names.

"I must try this way," she said. "It seems my best chance to be legally free of him—and truly safe." When she turned to face him, though, her heart misgave her. "The worst part is that your name will be dragged through the mud. You

would be better off without a woman who will bring you no-
toriety. Perhaps it's unwise of me to want a divorce at all."
"Now, now, my future bride." He took her left hand in
his and kissed the finger that wore the garnet ring they had
purchased from a secondhand shop. "We two are practically one now, remember? Nothing that affects your safety
or happiness is dispensable for me. Besides," he added, putting his arms around her, "you wouldn't deny me the
chance to stand up for you and prove my worthiness, would
you?"

That made her laugh, and she rested her head against
his shoulder, being careful not to dislodge the wig. "Your
worthiness isn't in question, Rob. Far from it." Then
she sighed. "I am so sorry to involve you in all this," she
said, for what she knew must be the dozenth or hundredth
time.

And as with all the previous times, Rob refused to let her
reproach herself. "You aren't to blame for being vulnerable
to a clever charlatan, Eleanor. This man is a professional
liar and manipulator. His fixing upon you was not your
fault, nor was your honorable nature at fault for being unable to see how vile he really is." He kissed her, and the
warmth of his touch in addition to the conviction of his
words gave her strength.

Standing up straighter, she smiled at him. "If I was mon-
strously unlucky in meeting him, at least I have been as
lucky in the opposite direction in meeting you." She
smoothed down his velvet Cavalier-style doublet. Rob was
dressed as Charles II, with a full-bottomed wig and broad-
brimmed plumed hat, so that his beard seemed part of his
disguise. "Now, I shall try to be braver, and soon enough
this will all be behind us."

"Amen," Rob said. "And don't forget, I am beside you in
this and in everything that comes, Eleanor."

She squeezed his hand. "I won't forget," she said. They said little on the journey to Sterne House. She was too preoccupied, and he must have sensed that small talk would only fret her nerves. He was wise about things like that, which made him surprisingly easy to live and work with. She felt a rush of gratitude for him and stretched up to kiss his cheek just before they walked up to the brilliantly illuminated entrance to the house.

Inside, they were relieved of their wraps and ushered downstairs to a small arched passage of concrete—the way to the ballroom. It was narrow and dark, perhaps a deliberate choice to make the scene when they emerged all the more dramatic.

And dramatic it certainly was. Dazzling gaslight lit up a dome of glass panes knitted together in a metal framework, with the panes shaped to narrow at the top, where a mighty chandelier was suspended. Benches and side tables were upholstered in plush green velvet, and in the center of the large table where the collation would be served stood a mermaid sculpture. One area had been partitioned off with potted palms, behind which an orchestra played.

"Astonishing," Rob said beneath his breath. "And all paid for with your money."

"One certainly can't fault him for lack of vision," she murmured. It was a little overwhelming, especially since she was going to have to confront the man who had been her husband—who still was, at least according to the law—and endure his fury. And in front of all these strangers! There must have been almost a hundred guests, plus the staff and musicians. Her heart hammered against her ribs so hard that she half expected to see the lace ruffle at her bosom vibrating.

Fortunately Cecily found them soon. Though masked like everyone else, she was unmistakable, and Eleanor felt cheered at the sight of so much youthful excitement and energy.

"I am so glad you came," she exclaimed, pressing Eleanor's hand. "I feared you wouldn't."

"I nearly changed my mind," she admitted. "But I know this is the best and safest way—for you as well as me."

Cecily nodded. Her silver half mask sparkled in the light. "I confess I feel my time is running short. That is my intended successor, there." She nodded toward a tall, poised young woman in the costume of Elizabeth I. Despite the lightness of her tone, Eleanor realized that there was tension beneath Cecily's energy.

"Does she know what he intends?" she asked.

"Gracious, I shouldn't think so. She seems too high-minded to condone a murder plot. Now, as to the timing, I thought perhaps midnight, when everyone unmasks."

Rob grimaced. "That will certainly be the most dramatic time."

"Oh, but don't you see, the orchestra will stop playing then, and if we wait just a minute for the hubbub to die down, Eleanor stands the best chance of making herself heard."

Eager to have the matter settled, Eleanor said, "That will be fine. What shall we do until then?"

"Why, dance," Cecily said. "It's the best way of blending in."

"I never cared much for dancing," Eleanor muttered, but Cecily had already darted away to greet other guests. Perhaps anxiety was making it hard for her to stand still for long.

To Eleanor's surprise, Rob took her hand and drew her toward the center of the room, where other couples were already waltzing. "I've always wanted to dance with you," he said, and behind his black mask his blue eyes were steady. He wasn't afraid, or at least he wasn't showing it, and that made her feel a little braver.

"You have?" she asked, as he placed one hand on her waist and led her into the dance.

"Do you remember the night last December when we were kept out late by an influenza case, and it snowed while we were with the patient? When we stepped out into the road, everything was white under the moonlight, and that old man on the corner was playing a concertina—"

"I do remember!" At the recollection she gave a little laugh. "I was cold and wanted to hurry home, but you said you wished to linger and listen to him playing."

His smile was as relaxed and warm as if they were safe at home by the fire instead of in the lair of the enemy. "How I wished I could have told you to set down your medical bag, take my hand, and dance with me on the pavement while the snow fell on us."

"What a romantic you are. I never would have dreamed it when we first met."

"I wasn't like this when we first met. I had little patience for anything but my work." He drew her close so he could say his next words into her ear. "You have been the making of me, Eleanor."

But the recollection of their first meeting, in that very same house, sobered Eleanor and chased her brief contentment away. If things should go wrong, she could end up shackled to Connor once more. The scandal could ruin Rob's career, and who knew what violent accident might befall Eleanor herself if she was forced to live under the same roof as her husband again?

The hours before midnight passed in that exhausting fashion, alternating between tense anxiety and brief interludes in which Rob helped her forget the night's errand. Sometimes she felt she was in a strange, hallucinatory dream, full of whirling masked couples dressed in everything from monks' robes to the phantasmagoria of Shakespeare's fairies. The music and conversation grew ever louder, ringing against the glass dome, beyond which the shifting dark waters could be glimpsed.

As midnight neared, she found concealment by the potted palms and stood trying to gather her strength. Her hands were visibly shaking, and Rob viewed her with concern.

"You need something to settle your nerves."

She shook her head. "I don't want any spirits. I need to keep a clear head."

"Very well, but I don't want you to become overheated in this crush. Will you be all right if I leave you alone long enough to fetch you some punch?"

Afraid to speak for fear her voice would tremble, she nodded. With one last troubled glance at her face, Rob strode away toward the refreshments.

Eleanor realized that Cecily was only a short distance away—not dancing, but deep in conversation with a man Eleanor did not recognize. He was dressed in the knee breeches and powdered wig of an 18th-century courtier, and he had succeeded in angering his hostess to the point that her mask could not hide her flushed cheeks and snapping eyes.

"—the most idiotic, dangerous thing you could possibly do!" she was hissing at him. "Have you stopped to think what will happen if he recognizes you?"

"I don't care." The reply was defiant and sounded like a young man's voice. "He must be made to answer for what he has done, Cecily. I ought to call him out."

Cecily's laugh was slightly overwrought. "That is just what we need to make the evening complete. Please promise me you'll do nothing of the sort."

"But someone must defend your honor."

"Now is not the time!"

Eleanor could not hear the young man's reply. Just then Rob reappeared with her drink. Unflappable though he was, even he was showing some tension. "Nearly time now," he said, his voice tight.

She drank, and the cool punch refreshed her. "Do you know the young man Cecily was speaking with?" she asked.

Rob looked around, but now the couple was nowhere to be seen. "Is it important?"

"Perhaps not." She needed to gather her thoughts. The music was racing toward a peak, and when it reached it a tall, broad-shouldered man stepped forward.

Connor. All night she had caught brief glimpses of him but immediately averted her eyes, reluctant both to call attention to herself and to think too deeply about this man. The memories were too troublingly mixed. There was some happiness there, and even pleasure, and that made the fear and sense of betrayal all the worse. Perhaps the most difficult thing was that even now she could not hate him. It would have been easier, she felt, if she could have hated him.

Now he held up his hands to silence the crowd, and the orchestra brought their tune to a close. Expectant faces turned toward the host, and Cecily appeared at his side, still masked.

"Welcome, all of you," he announced, his voice carrying without effort. "This ball is just the first of what I hope will become a Sterne House tradition. Tomorrow you can tell your friends that you danced beneath a lake!" There was a ripple of appreciative laughter, and Connor reached out to draw Cecily closer. "Now comes that amusing part of the evening when everyone unmasks. My wife and I will lead the way."

He untied the ribbon that held Cecily's mask on, and her face when revealed was still and serious. She had just untied his in turn, and Eleanor was steeling herself to come forward, when a voice shouted, "Imposter!"

The young man who had been speaking so urgently with Cecily strode forward, tearing off his mask. "You married Cecily under false pretenses," he accused. "You are not the real Connor Blake."

As closely as Eleanor was watching Connor, she thought she saw him start. But he recovered quickly and countered, "It seems there is an interloper in our midst. What right do you have to intrude here with such wild accusations?"

"I come here with Cecily's interests at heart. I love her, and that gives me the right to challenge you."

Cecily gave a little groan. "Freddie, do be quiet!"

But he plunged on recklessly. "I also have whatever rights are conferred by this," he said, drawing a pistol from somewhere in his costume and pointing it at Connor.

Eleanor's stomach hollowed out in dread. There were exclamations and a few cries of alarm from the women guests.

"Good God," Rob muttered. "There is no way this will end well."

Eleanor wondered feverishly what would happen if a bullet were to strike the glass dome. Could the glass withstand a shot? Or would they all be drowned—or crushed beneath the dome if it collapsed?

Connor's face had darkened with rage. "You dare to bring a weapon into my house?" he demanded, striding over to the now shocked young man and wrenching the gun from his grasp. "I should have you horsewhipped." He raised the gun as though he were about to strike the young man with it, and Eleanor stepped forward quickly, fumbling her mask off.

"Connor, leave him be," she said. Now that the moment had come, she felt strangely calm. "He is of no consequence."

At the sound of her voice, her husband's face went slack with dread. His dark eyes were haunted when they found her, and then he seemed to shrink away.

"Eleanor?" It was barely audible. "You're—dead."

"Yes," she said. "So you were meant to think. I left you because I feared for my life, and now I must make certain you don't—"

But before she could finish the sentence, Connor gave a hoarse cry.

"You should have stayed dead."

He raised the pistol with a shaking hand. Behind her, Rob swore. Cecily and Freddie looked on in horror, and then the gun fired.

There was so much noise and motion at first that Eleanor's mind was confused. Gaily dressed revelers, shouting in their panic, rushed to the two exit passages. But she had not fallen and felt no pain anywhere. Had he missed her?

Rob was suddenly grasping her shoulders, turning her so that his body was a shield between her and the man with the pistol. "Are you all right?" he demanded, sending a quick, searching glance over her from head to foot.

"I—I believe so. I don't think he hit me."

Connor must have come to the same conclusion, for he raised the gun again. Freddie reached out to try to seize it at the same moment that a loud, brittle sound cut through the noise of the room.

Cecily gasped and pointed. "The glass—the shot broke the glass!"

The crack was visible for only a moment. Almost at once the pressure of the water burst the pane inward, and the force was enough to bend the metal framework and shatter more glass. With a metallic groan the dome began to collapse, bowing under the weight of the onrushing water. Screams sounded as those who had not yet made their way out tried frantically to squeeze past those in their path.

Water was pouring in at such a rate that it knocked Connor and Cecily off their feet. Rob took Eleanor's hands, steadying her as the rising water swirled about their waists. He was pale. She knew she must be as well.

"We shall have to swim for it," he said, raising his voice to be heard over the rushing of water and the cries of fear. The two exit passages seemed to be jammed. Perhaps the crush of people was too great. Now the water had reached their shoulders. "Eleanor," Rob said urgently, "if we should be—"

His words were cut off as the water surged higher. Then she was wrenched away, and their hands were torn apart. The dark water bore her up toward the gaping hole in the mangled dome.

Sound was muted as the water engulfed her, and her mind was suddenly taken back to the night of her supposed death. The feeling of the water carrying her, the current too strong to withstand, swept over her in one frightening instant.

On that long-ago night she had forced herself to let the current take her, trusting it to carry her where she needed to go. Tonight she saw the moon above, kicked her legs, and swam toward it.

CHAPTER FIFTEEN
Cecily

Cecily breached the surface with a grateful intake of breath. All around was chaos—people swimming, thrashing, crying out. She did not see Connor anywhere.

Somehow she reached the shore and staggered out of the water, her clothes streaming. She had lost her crown and her shoes, and had to cough up a fair quantity of disgusting water, but no matter. She was alive.

Everything had happened so quickly. She could hardly believe that Connor had grown desperate enough to try to murder Eleanor, and before so many people. She shuddered. Her last glimpse of him had been of his wild-eyed face under the coral crown as the water swept his feet out from under him.

The level of the lake had sunk by several feet, making it easier for people to find their footing and clamber onto dry land. With a rush of relief that almost dizzied her, she caught sight of Eleanor. She was nearly unrecognizable in her white wig, which had lost all its curl and streamed down over her shoulders, making her look like a witch. She was tending to a man who lay prone on the ground, feeling his head for injuries. Even now, she was thinking of others.

As Cecily watched, Dr. Grant came into view. He, too, was soaking, but he had lost his hat and wig and so looked at least somewhat normal. The moment that he saw

Eleanor he ran to draw her to her feet and embrace her, but almost at once she began to speak and motion toward the man on the ground. The doctor released her with an air of reluctance but then knelt by the prostrate man to tend to him.

The sight made Cecily smile. Then she shivered. The night air was chilly against her wet skin and hair—and she did not know what had happened to Connor. Considering how recklessly he had behaved, she would not feel safe until she knew where he was.

"Mrs. Blake? What has happened?" Mrs. Ansley came hurrying up, looking all around in horrified fascination. Of course—she had not been present in the ballroom.

"There has been an accident," she said, aware of how insufficient an explanation it was. But this was not the time to go into the details. "If you would be so good as to alert any other servants who can help—especially any who can swim—that would be most helpful."

"I will, madam." She hesitated a moment, scanning the tumultuous scene before her. "Did the master...has he emerged yet?"

"Not yet." Cecily's eyes met hers. "Some lanterns would be of great help. And you might ask Eleanor if she and the doctor need any supplies."

The housekeeper gave a brief nod in reply, then went to confer briefly with Eleanor and Dr. Grant before hastening back to the house. Cecily continued to scan the chaotic scene. Few now were left to fend for themselves in the water; stronger swimmers were assisting weaker ones. She saw Freddie helping Augusta Norris to shore, perhaps the first useful thing he had done that evening. He looked up at that moment and saw her, and his eyes lit up. With ungallant speed he abandoned Miss Norris and half ran to Cecily.

"Don't," she said, as soon as he had come within hearing range, an apology clearly on his lips. "Have you seen Connor?"

He hesitated. "As far as I can tell, no one has seen him." Cecily shuddered again, and Freddie shucked off his jacket as though to offer it to her before realizing that, soaked with lake water as it was, it would not do her a whit of good.

She realized that the best thing she could do at the moment was to busy herself seeing to her guests and trying to make certain they were as comfortable as possible. Though she had no material comforts to offer, she made herself pass among the survivors and try to give them some kind of reassurance.

Soon bobbing lights showed that servants were arriving with lanterns. Some carried a small rowboat, which they launched in search of anyone still in the water. Two of the youngest footmen, who had emerged from the wreckage unscathed, were already diving beneath the surface while others held lanterns.

They retrieved three bodies in all. Two were unfortunate guests, an elderly man and woman who must not have been strong enough to swim to safety. The other was the master of the house.

"His cape was caught, madam," Janet came to tell Cecily presently. The maid's voice was hushed with the importance of her errand. "Otherwise he might have been able to escape and swim to the surface with everyone else. I'm sorry to have to give you such dreadful news, madam."

Cecily's legs gave out, and she sat down hard on the muddy ground. Connor could no longer harm her—or anyone. She was free of him, the man who had been her husband yet not her husband.

Eleanor needs to know, she thought. Through numb lips she said, "Thank you, Janet. Please go tell the nurse—the lady in the pink dress, over there."

The maid curtseyed, and Cecily watched as she went all unknowing to speak to the first Mrs. Blake. Then she saw Eleanor impulsively fling her arms around first the maid, then Dr. Grant.

Cecily's heart lifted a little. Eleanor no longer had to live in fear. She could reclaim her property and, more important, her freedom.

"Cecily, I'm awfully sorry." She found Freddie at her side again, extending his hand to help her up. His stricken expression made her think of a scolded puppy. "Can you ever forgive me? I can't help feeling that this wouldn't have happened without me."

He was almost certainly right. But she hadn't the heart to lecture him now, when he could see all around him the consequences of his rashness.

What she really wanted to do was to go indoors, shed her wet costume, and warm herself by a roaring fire. But she had to be lady of the manor for a little while longer, and that meant she had to see to everyone else's needs before her own. How happy she would be to relinquish that role to Eleanor, she realized.

Then a hush began to creep over the noisy scene. Cecil found two of the footmen carrying a body toward her. They had draped his cape over him, but she knew it was Connor. Gently they lowered him to the ground, and then they waited.

She realized she was expected to do something.

Uncomfortably aware that everyone was watching, she drew toward the still form, and the servants fell back to give her room. Kneeling by the draped body, she drew back the fabric that covered its face.

It was Connor, his eyes still open and staring. It was perfectly clear that he was dead, but she looked up and called, "Doctor?" to summon Dr. Grant and Eleanor.

The doctor came and felt for a pulse at his neck, then his wrist. He put his ear to the dead man's chest and listened, then shook his head at Cecily.

Eleanor had been watching closely. When the doctor shook his head she, too, knelt by the body. Her face was unreadable as, with a steady hand, she closed his eyelids. Connor Blake—or James Snow—was dead.

The next few days were unpleasant. Speaking to the local authorities, the survivors, the servants, and the family of those who had not survived—the last were the worst, and she felt miserably guilty even though she had had no part in the deaths. She tried to protect Freddie by telling the authorities that she thought her husband was the one who had brought the gun, but she knew others had seen Freddie produce it.

"At least you were able to cast doubt on their story," he told her when he came to call. "I haven't been arrested, and that is the main thing." Uninvited, he seated himself next to Cecily on the divan. They were in the parlor, where Cecily had hoped to spend a quiet and solitary afternoon writing letters.

"I'm glad of that," she said politely. She was wearing black, as she supposed she ought to do in order to keep up the appearance of being a widow until Eleanor's lawyers revealed the sensational truth and the public at large learned of the bigamous marriage. The servants all knew by this time, but it was clear that the news had not reached Freddie.

"You will also be glad to know that I've found out when and how your husband became Connor Blake," he said, and if his air was more than a little cocky, Cecily felt it was understandable in the circumstances.

"Really?" she exclaimed. "What have you discovered?"

In the face of her interest Freddie preened a bit. "It seems that James Snow was valet to the real Connor Blake. When Blake was killed at Inkerman, Snow took the opportunity to switch clothes and identities with him."

"Good heavens! However did he manage to fool anyone into accepting him as Blake?"

"There was some physical resemblance, remember. And who better to learn a man's habits and mannerisms than his valet?"

"And I suppose the chaos of battle made it easier for him to go undetected," Cecily mused. "How extraordinary."

"Exactly. It was only by chance that my acquaintance at the club was watching when the real Blake was cut down on the field." He sat back, beaming.

"You have done quite well, Freddie," she said, since he clearly expected it. Indeed, it was intriguing knowledge, and she must share it with Eleanor. "And now that you have helped me so much, you may rejoin your family with a clear conscience, wherever they are at present."

But he did not recognize her words as the dismissal they were meant to be. "Speaking of my family," he said, with an even greater air of importance and pent-up excitement than before, "I have managed to wear them down. They are willing to accept you as my wife! Isn't that wonderful news?"

She gave him a puzzled look. "Your wife? What are you talking about?"

His laugh was just a trifle condescending. "Why, our marriage, of course. Now we are free to wed. After a suitable mourning period, of course. Aren't you delighted?"

There was a time when she would have been, that was true. But that time seemed far distant, coming as it had before her marriage to Connor and her life as the mistress of Sterne House, not to mention the interval during which her husband was revealed not to be her husband at all. It seemed like another Cecily altogether who had fancied herself in love with this boy—for a boy was all he was to her, despite the new hints of maturity she had glimpsed recently.

Her silence had made him anxious. "Cecily?"

"I don't think you will still want to marry me when you learn the whole truth," she said. "You see, my marriage to Connor—or James—was never legal or sanctified. His previous wife was alive the entire time, though I didn't know it until recently."

"Alive?" he repeated, looking as confused and disoriented as though he had walked into a post.

"She was at the ball, in fact. She has been using the name Jones."

She felt a bit sorry for him. He was trying valiantly not to let his face fall, but his eyes were shocked and his complexion sickly pale. She wondered if she should ring for smelling salts.

"You needn't worry," she said gently. "I shan't force you to marry me. Under the circumstances, it would be heartless to make you go through with it."

Now it was his turn to look puzzled. "What do you mean?"

"Well, in your eyes I must look a bit soiled. Being a widow without having been a bride, you know. I don't blame you for retracting your offer."

"I retract nothing," he retorted, rearing back to regard her with a kind of astonished reproach. "You are still Cecily, and I still love you and want to protect you."

She hid a wry smile. It was doubtful that she would ever need to be protected against anything as bad as what had already befallen her.

He added hotly, "I would never consider you soiled—detestable term." Then he diminished the valiant effect of his words by adding, "However, it would be best all around if we could prevent my parents from learning of this—er—development."

She had to give him credit for his faithfulness. In that respect he had certainly improved since ending their engagement. But in a way it made things more difficult for her.

"As much as I appreciate your willingness to stand by me, Freddie," she said, "the fact is that I don't wish to marry you. But thank you for asking."

That pricked his pride. "Don't be preposterous, Cecily. You must live somehow, and now—pardon me for pointing it out—no other respectable person will marry you."

"That's just it," she said with as much patience as she could muster. "It isn't you that I don't want to marry. I don't want to marry anyone at all."

This seemed to baffle him. "But you must want children."

"I suppose I might, someday. But not now. The truth is that I have had enough of marriage. Yes, even though I was not wedded in the eyes of God or the courts, it was a close enough imitation—and I don't envision myself wanting any more of it for quite a while, perhaps never."

Having to give up what little independence she had had, living out her days according to the moods of a man, being forced into subterfuge to avoid his temper—she wanted no more of it. Even a man who seemed more docile, like Freddie, would expect to rule his household, and she could imagine how often she would have to soothe his feelings to keep harmony in the household.

"No," she said, with finality. "Marriage is not for me."

She could see him trying to take in this idea. Matrimonially speaking, he was a catch—and knew it, now that he had stood up to his parents and gained their permission...and, more crucially, their financial support. He was handsome, healthy, of good family, free of the obvious vices, and likely to be a kind husband and indulgent father.

He also represented the most boring future Cecily could imagine.

"But what on earth will you do?" he demanded. "Forgive my bluntness, but women in your situation haven't many wholesome ways to live."

Had her circumstances been the same as before her marriage, Cecily would have been more worried about that herself. But Eleanor in her generosity had promised that, no matter how Cecily chose to live her life, she could always rely on having a home.

"Perhaps I shall train as a nurse," she said, wondering if Eleanor could help her overcome her distaste for the messier parts of that type of work. "Or I might become a novelist. One needn't be respectable to do that. Being an actress might be amusing, with my experience in dissembling." She eyed Freddie and considered telling him that letting his mouth hang open like that, especially while his eyes were bugged out in astonishment, gave him an unpleasant resemblance to a fish. Then she decided it would be unkind.

"I shall find something," she said. "I might even be a lady's maid to Eleanor, if she should decide to leave nursing and become a grand lady. She can certainly afford to now."

He was silent for a moment, then seemed to accept defeat. He rose and stood before her, in a new dignity not entirely spoiled by his ridiculous light blue checked suit, which did not suit him as well as his rusticated disguise. "You must do what is best for you, Cecily," he said. "Only please remember that you may call on me if ever you are in need."

"Thank you," she said, matching his solemnity. "I shall remember that."

She rang for a servant to bring his hat and gloves and walked with him to the front door when he departed. He kissed her hand and gazed at her earnestly, but when she did not relent he walked slowly down the front stairs.

Watching him make his way down the path, skirting the lake and its wreckage, she felt strangely light. It was as though only now was the trouble of the past truly behind her.

She waved at him, then went back inside and shut the door. She found Cousin Margaret in the housekeeper's parlor, demonstrating a new embroidery technique to Mrs. Ansley.

"Has he finally gone, dear?" her cousin asked her.

With a sigh, Cecily took a seat in the rocking chair. The little parlor was crowded with the three of them, but it was the coziest place in the house. "He was rather a lamb after all," she said. "Quite maddening, of course, but I think he may yet make some woman a decent husband."

"But not you?"

"Not I." She rocked and thought for a bit. "I suppose I ought to have another talk with Eleanor. We've not really spoken since she said that I could send for you and that we two could stay here for the time being. I ought to start making plans."

"I suppose she's busy, between the legal matters and planning the wedding."

"That reminds me," the housekeeper said, half to herself. "I need to make certain Cook hasn't forgotten the sauce for the Nesselrode pudding. And that the best table linens have been laundered."

"I thought the wedding breakfast was to be a modest affair," Cecily said. "Isn't that why Eleanor didn't want it at Sterne House but at your mother-in-law's cottage?"

Mrs. Ansley gave her a knowing look. "I think it is safe to say that there are many reasons Mrs. Blake didn't want to celebrate her wedding at Sterne House. But that doesn't mean we cannot offer the guests a fine spread."

Cecily thought about the life that lay ahead for Eleanor. From what Cecily knew of her, the soon-to-be Mrs. Grant was likely to continue her nursing. She would probably sell Sterne House, and who could blame her? Doubtless she would have her hospital built, and she and the handsome doctor would work side by side saving lives until eventually they would be awarded honors by the queen herself.

Unfortunately Cecily felt no such calling. Thanks to Eleanor, though, she had security. This time she would be spared the indignity and desperation of grasping at whatever offer came her way. Indeed, Eleanor had saved her twice. Without her intervention, Cecily might soon have fallen victim to her—*their*—unscrupulous husband. And now she had the freedom to decide for herself what to do with her future. The possibilities stretched before her.

"You're very quiet, dear," Cousin Margaret said. "Building castles in the air?"

Cecily smiled. "I've had enough of castles," she said. "What I'm building is a road."

CHAPTER SIXTEEN
Eleanor

C onnor Blake's body floated in the submerged wreckage of the ballroom, his dark hair wafting like seaweed in the water, his eyes wide and staring as if looking for the next opportunity for advancement. Small silver fish nibbled at his eyelids and darted in and out of his gaping mouth. His flesh was pale with a greenish cast in the light that filtered down through the water. And then one bloated hand shot out and seized Eleanor by the throat.

That was the picture that haunted her dreams for many nights following the ball. When she woke to Rob's presence, her heart always welled with gratitude. She drew both comfort and strength from him when he held her close, and she knew that the dreams would eventually go away altogether...when she finally truly believed that the man she had known as Connor Blake was no longer able to harm her.

Today the remnants of the dream were easily sloughed away because of what lay ahead. She and Rob rose early, and shortly after dawn they were dressed and ready to embark upon the day.

He was wearing his best suit, a dark blue frock coat and matching trousers, and carried new gloves and a polished silk hat. His brown hair was combed carefully back from his brow, and his beard was freshly trimmed. When he smiled at her, the endearing crinkles at the corners of his eyes showed.

"Have you everything you need?" he asked.

She was wearing a dress that Mrs. Ansley had brought to her from the belongings she had left behind in Sterne House. It was one she had never worn during her marriage, so it had no unhappy associations. Made of a coppery silk taffeta, it had a flounced skirt embroidered with tiny ivy leaves. There was ivory galloon lace at the neck and wrists, and at her throat was the brooch set with seed pearls that her father had given her on her fourteenth birthday. Rob had not parted with it after she impulsively forced it on him that day at old Mrs. Ansley's cottage, and one of his first acts when she had begun her new life as his nurse had been to restore it to her.

"Let's see," she said. "The something old is my brooch from Papa. The something new is the hat. Borrowed—the handkerchief from Cecily."

"And the blue?"

She stepped closer to him and slipped her arms around his neck. "I don't suppose my bridegroom's beautiful blue eyes count."

"Probably not," he said with a chuckle, wrapping his arms around her, and kissed her until she nearly forgot the question.

"Something blue," he prompted when he released her at last.

"Oh—yes." Under his fond gaze she straightened her hat, knowing she was blushing. "Now I remember. Mrs. Ansley embroidered a corset cover with blue forget-me-nots."

"Ah, yes, I caught a glimpse of that while you were dressing. Very fetching. And the final item, the silver sixpence in your shoe?"

She drew back her skirt so that the toes of her russet leather boots showed. "I stitched it into the bow on my right boot. It was just too uncomfortable inside. You don't think that will take away from our luck in married life, do you?"

The expression in his eyes told her that they would not need luck, because they had everything else a man and woman could give each other. Ardent love, friendship, a common passion in their work; respect, laughter, patience; and a community of friends, who just now were gathering at old Mrs. Ansley's cottage in preparation for the wedding breakfast and who would help them weather whatever rough patches lay ahead.

"And money," Cecily had pointed out when Eleanor had voiced these thoughts to her the day before. "Money is bound to make things easier. That, and being widowed."

"It is indeed advantageous to be widowed before remarrying," Eleanor had said with a straight face, and Cecily had stuck out her tongue at her. Cecily was going to be her bridesmaid. She had not yet decided on her next steps, but at eighteen years old she had plenty of time in which to consider. Eleanor, who had conceived a sisterly fondness for her, was ready to assist her in whatever she next proposed to do.

Rob took her hand, bringing her back to the present moment. "I think we shall do quite well," he said, smiling. "Are you ready, Eleanor?"

She squeezed his hand. "Ready," she said, and with him at her side she stepped out the door and into their future.

The End

About the Author

Amanda DeWees received her PhD in English from the University of Georgia and wrote her dissertation on 19th-century vampire literature—the perfect training, although she didn't know it at the time, for writing Victorian gothic romance novels. Her books include *With This Curse*, winner of the 2015 Daphne du Maurier Award in historical mystery/suspense, and the Sybil Ingram Victorian Mysteries series. Visit her at AmandaDeWees.com to learn more.